A Warning?

"What is it, Gerry?" she asked. "Is anything the matter?"

"I've finished the crossword but for two clues," he replied in the most mundane of tones. "Perhaps you will have an inspiration."

And he read out the clues. Dorothy instantly supplied one of the solutions. The word was "murder." As soon as she said it, she felt that little shiver of fear again. He had wanted her to say the word "murder." Was this some new sort of blackmail? A hint that he proposed to accuse her openly of murder or attempted murder? Or was it a warning that she might herself be in danger from him?

"What was the other clue again?" she asked . . .

ANNA CLARKE

ONE OF US MUST DIE

CHARTER BOOKS, NEW YORK

This Charter book contains the complete
text of the original hardcover edition.
It has been completely reset in a typeface
designed for easy reading, and was printed
from new film.

ONE OF US MUST DIE

A Charter Book/published by arrangement with
Doubleday, a division of Bantam, Doubleday,
Dell Publishing Group, Inc.

PRINTING HISTORY
Doubleday edition published 1980
Charter edition/August 1988

ISBN: 1-55773-059-8

Charter Books are published by The Berkley Publishing Group,
200 Madison Avenue, New York, New York 10016.
The name ''Charter'' and the ''C'' logo
are trademarks belonging to Charter Communications, Inc.

PRINTED IN THE UNITED STATES OF AMERICA

10   9   8   7   6   5   4   3   2   1

1

"Gerry! Where are you?"

Dr. Dorothy Laver pushed open the door of the sitting-room of Pond Cottage, Middle Lane, Hampstead. It was a pleasant blue-and-white room with long windows opening on to a balcony over which trailed a pale clematis in full flower on this June morning. Two daily papers were lying crumpled on the carpet by the side of an armchair and the ashtray was full of cigarette ends, but there was no sign of her husband. Half an hour ago she had telephoned from the hospital to say that she would be home to lunch. Gerry had seemed all right then and had promised to have a drink ready for her. Either he had been putting on an act or one of his attacks had come on very suddenly.

Dr. Laver emerged from the sitting-room and looked into the little study at the back of the house where Gerry gave English lessons to private pupils from a tutorial college when he was well enough.

This room, too, was empty, but Dorothy's quick and anxious glance instantly picked out the sheet of writing-paper on the desk. It was lying on the blotter at a slight angle and the thin ballpoint pen lay beside it as if the writer

1

had been suddenly called away but intended to return. Only a few lines had been written in Gerry's small neat hand.

> My darling Dolly, I can no longer endure to be such a burden to you. I must once again take steps to end it, and this time I promise I will not fail. By the time you return it will all be over and you will be free of me for ever and can marry any one of them you choose or enjoy the house with your lover in peace . . .

Dr. Laver took in the contents of the letter with no change of expression on her face, but as she left the room there was the slight tensing of the hand muscles with which she always prepared herself to meet an emergency, whether it was a domestic crisis or a particularly difficult patient at hospital.

Her hands were clenched into fists when she looked into the kitchen and the downstairs lavatory and her own consulting-room and saw no Gerry. This meant that he would be upstairs. An ominous sign and she feared the worst. The messiest and the most thoroughly upsetting kind. Fortunately it was also the rarest. He had only once before done it this way. Her own telephone call had probably sparked it off. Knowing for sure that she would very soon be home he had felt safe in doing this. Or perhaps he had waited until he saw her car actually turn into Middle Lane. The bathroom was at the front of the house and there was a good view of the road from the window.

Dorothy Laver picked up her emergency bag before she ran upstairs. She would almost certainly need it. When she reached the turn of the stairs she heard sounds of groaning. Timed just right, she said to herself. It was extraordinary how she could be logical and aloof, deeply compassionate, guilty, and just plain scared all at the same time. You'd think you'd get used to it, she thought as she reached the bathroom door. After all, it must be the tenth—or was it the eleventh?—time.

Deliberately she set herself the task of counting the previous suicide attempts. The little mental exercise reinforced the coldly rational part of herself and helped to steady her while she staunched the flow of blood, cleaned the slashed wrists, and put in the stitches. He had used a new razor blade and the cuts were straight and not very deep. The repair job was a simple enough one in itself. Dorothy Laver practised now as a psychiatrist, but she had not lost her basic skills. What was so agonizing to her was not the gushing blood but the sickening stream of self-reproach that flowed from Gerry's lips while she was dressing the wounds.

"Why do you bother, why don't you just let me die . . . I'm not worth it . . . I'm a misery to you . . . I always will be . . . I've ruined your life . . . and you're so wonderful, Dolly, so strong, so good."

And so on and so on. Drowning in self-pity, pouring out the old clichés over and over again, luxuriating in it. These were now the high spots, the greatest times in his life. It would not be quite so bad if he were no more than a weak hysterical creature who was completely dependent on her and whom she could treat as she treated her patients. Compassion and professional pride would carry her through. And it would be easier to bear if he truly loved her in spite of everything, if they were tied together with bonds of past affection instead of with hatred and guilt. For it was his hatred that was so hard to bear, his bitter resentment of her that was never openly expressed but always indirectly in these carefully timed and arranged suicide attempts. He had got it down to a fine art, she reflected as she scrubbed round the bathroom floor tiles to remove the remaining traces of blood. He knew her moods and weaknesses, her likes and dislikes. Being a doctor, she was all the more vulnerable. He tortured her conscience with these fake suicide bids as an experienced kidnapper or hijacker played on the conscience of a civilized society.

And her conscience was terribly sore, sore with a wound that would never heal, sore in a way that nobody else knew about except Gerry.

"How are you feeling now?" she asked him a few minutes later.

Gerry Laver was lying on his bed in his olive-green dressing-gown, propped up against an edifice of pillows. On the bedside table stood a transistor radio tuned softly to Radio One and a small tray containing a whisky bottle and a jug of water. In the less damaged of his hands he held a cigarette and with the other he was rather awkwardly turning the pages of the morning's *Guardian* which was propped against his knees. He looked as elegant and placid and comfortable as the hero of a Noel Coward play.

"Fine," he replied, looking up and smiling at her. "Thanks to my clever darling Dolly."

It was indeed as if he were acting to an unseen audience. But he was not forcing her into any particular role. She had played her part and given him his satisfaction by being unable to conceal her own horror and revulsion, and he was no longer interested in her. At any rate not for the time being. Later on—it might be a week, it might be a fortnight, it might even, with great luck, be two or three months—the whole disgusting business would start again and there was nothing whatever that she could do to prevent it.

"Do you want any lunch?" Dorothy was so exhausted by the struggle within her that she had barely enough strength to ask the question. For a moment it looked as if she would have to repeat it because Gerry, seemingly completely absorbed in something he was reading, took no notice. Just when she could stand it no longer he shifted slightly and murmured without looking up. "Later. Not just yet. I'll have a little something later on." And then he laughed, quite naturally and happily as he read from the paper, "Listen to this, darling. Man pours bucket of ice cubes over wife's lover. He's up in court for causing grievous bodily harm. How could you cause harm with ice cubes? It might cool his ardour and he'd probably get very wet, but otherwise . . ."

Dorothy heard no more. Her own impulse to attack Gerry could no longer be held in check and the violence of it horrified her. It had never been as bad as this before. She rushed out of the bedroom, just remembering to leave the door open in case he should call her, but not knowing how she would be able to respond if he did.

In the pretty blue-and-white sitting-room she walked up and down until she was a little calmer and then swallowed a little white tablet and sat down on the settee, breathing deeply and commanding herself not to think about Gerry until the tranquillizer had begun to take effect.

But it took a second tablet and a glass of sherry and the best part of an hour before relief came at last. Dorothy kicked off her shoes and lay back on the settee with her eyes closed. It was fortunate that she did not have to go back to hospital this afternoon and was not seeing any patient at home until four o'clock. Two hours to recover. She would sleep for an hour and then make tea and sandwiches for herself and Gerry and gradually get back into the normal routine.

But sleep did not come. The drug held her body in its grip like a strait-jacket but her thoughts had no such restraint. You can have your freedom from him, they kept telling her. It's terribly easy. All you have to do is to let it happen next time. Not to come to the rescue. To arrive home too late.

— 2 —

The front doorbell broke into Dorothy's waking nightmare. Upstairs, Gerry, drifting off into a comfortable doze, scarcely heard it. Dorothy smoothed down her hair and her skirt as she went to answer the ring and made an effort to appear her usual self. That it was not a very successful effort was immediately apparent from the reaction of the young man who stood on the doorstep.

"Good afternoon," he said. And then, apologetically, "I'm sorry to disturb you."

Dorothy tried a bit harder and achieved a little twitch of the lips that might pass for a smile.

"Not at all. What can I do for you?"

He doesn't look as if he's selling anything, she thought; he's not nearly brash enough. But perhaps it was a new technique. And she didn't recognize him as a patient, although it was not impossible that he was somebody whom she had seen briefly at the hospital and who, resentful of receiving so little time and despairing of ever coming to the top of the waiting list for treatment, had sought her out at her private address. Except that he didn't look like a patient either, and certainly not the type who would go to such lengths. He was of medium build and medium colouring, and he spoke with a slight West Country accent. Could he possibly be canvassing in the by-election, wondered Dorothy. Surely not. He didn't look right for that either.

"Is Mr. Laver in?" asked the caller, and Dorothy's dazed mental fumblings came to an end as she realized that it was Gerry who was wanted and not herself. She even experienced a momentary flicker of sympathy for Gerry, whom a few minutes ago she had been wishing dead. It was tough on him to be nearly always regarded as nothing more than an awkward appendage of his wife, as Dr. Laver's husband. If they separated he might just have a chance to recover and lead a normal life. Perhaps she ought to try, even now, really to talk to him. Perhaps if she were to admit her own deep feelings of guilt, for everything, not just that first disaster . . . perhaps if she could bring herself to take the plunge and open up the forbidden subject after all these years . . .

"I'm afraid Mr. Laver isn't very well at the moment," she said in a much firmer voice. "Was he expecting you?"

"At half past two," was the reply. "I have a tutorial arranged for then."

"Oh dear." Dorothy glanced at her watch. "What a pity that you've had a wasted journey. Are you one of his regular pupils? I'm Mrs. Laver, by the way."

"I'm Peter Tarrant." The young man suddenly held out his hand and Dorothy took it for a moment. "No, I'm not a regular student," he went on. "I've never seen Mr. Laver before. The agency fixed it up for me. I'd better go then, if he's not well, and perhaps I can see him another time."

"I'm awfully sorry," said Dorothy. "I hope you've not had very far to come."

That was obviously all that needed to be said in the circumstances and Peter Tarrant ought to have shut the door and returned to her own affairs. But neither of them did so. They remained staring at each other.

"Is he very ill?" asked Peter at last. "Is there anything I can do to help you?"

Dorothy made no reply. It was so rare for anybody to think that she could be in need of help that she was momentarily taken aback.

"I thought you looked very worried when you opened the door," said Peter. "I hope you don't think I'm being interfering, but I couldn't help noticing."

Suddenly Dorothy smiled, quite naturally, and the young man blinked. She was in her late thirties, he supposed, tall, thin, and rather frail-looking with short straight black hair and a pale skin. But her mouth, which was too large, and her eyes, which were violet-coloured and rather too close together for beauty, seemed to come alive when she smiled and fill her whole face with light and movement. If he had known the expression he would have called her a *belle laide*. As it was, he simply thought how extraordinarily fascinating a plain woman could sometimes look.

"It's nothing very serious," she said, "but he was taken ill rather suddenly and that's why he couldn't let you know in time. I was a bit dopey when you rang because I'd been resting and had just woken up and had not fully connected."

This brought another apology from Peter. Dorothy cut it short. She was feeling quite wide awake now and extraordinarily light-hearted all of a sudden. To be treated by this pleasant and sympathetic stranger not as Dr. Laver who was to be deferred to and depended on at every turn, but simply as an ordinary woman worried about her husband, had touched some deep spring of release in her. She felt irresponsible and free, as if she had been magically transported beyond the bounds of her own life and could show herself as whatever sort of person she pleased.

"I tell you what we will do, Peter Tarrant," she said. "I was just going to make some tea. You come in and wait while I do so, and I'll take some up to my husband and see whether he's fit to see you now for a little while. If he isn't, then perhaps I could help you a bit myself. I'm an idiot in some subjects but might be able to remember some useful tips in others. What do you need coaching in?"

Peter explained while they were in the kitchen, where he insisted on following her. He was trying to make up for an interrupted education by doing an Open University degree in Technology. The practical side did not worry him much, since he had worked at a variety of engineering jobs and was at the moment earning his living as an electrician, helping a friend who had a thriving one-man business. It was writing essays that was his problem.

"I've never been much good at getting things down on paper," he said as he was quickly and efficiently cutting bread and butter for the sandwiches. "It's all quite clear in my mind and I can explain it to somebody else if necessary, but I panic at the sight of a blank sheet of paper."

"That's not an uncommon experience," said Dorothy, laughing. "You're in good company. But surely the Open University ought to be helping you?"

"Oh, they are. They're super. My counsellor has spent hours with me, but I still feel I need more practice. I can't afford to fail."

"All the same, I don't think you ought to be spending money on private coaching," said Dorothy, suspecting that the agency that sent Gerry his pupils was making a very comfortable profit out of them.

"It would be even worse to have to take the course over again," returned Peter. "There. Will these do?"

"Much better than I'd have made myself. Thank you very much."

Dorothy put the sandwiches on a tray. "If you'd like to wait in here," she went on, indicating the sitting-room, "I'll go up and investigate. Shan't be long."

A little later she returned, still carrying the tray. "He's fast asleep," she said. "I won't wake him. Let's see if I can help you myself. I'm free till a quarter to four. Excuse me chewing and drinking the while."

It turned out that Peter had actually brought along an

exercise for comment and advice. It was a report to an imaginary board of directors, comparing the merits of rival pieces of office machinery. The technical details were admirably clear and the conclusions, though rather naïvely presented, gave ample information on which to form a judgement. Dorothy studied it carefully while Peter Tarrant poured tea and demolished the sandwiches as if he too had had nothing to eat all day.

"It's a lucky firm who gets you for technical adviser," she said at last, looking up from her reading and smiling at him. The pleasant, undistinguished face opposite her went very red.

"There's no need to be kind about it," he muttered, turning aside to put his cup down on the table. "I know I can't write."

"I'm not being kind about it," Dorothy exclaimed. "I'm telling you what I think. For what my opinion is worth, that is."

Peter looked up at her again and they glared at each other for a moment. Then they both said "Sorry" simultaneously and burst out laughing.

"As a matter of fact I've got rather a high opinion of my own opinion," said Dorothy. "Shall we cut out the false modesty all around and start again?"

"Yes, please." Peter took another sandwich. "I've got quite a good opinion of myself too. In some respects."

"What repects? Hi." Dorothy grabbed the plate. "Leave me something to eat, can't you?"

"I feel as if I've known you for years," said Peter. "Funny, isn't it? What respects? Well, I'm pretty good at diagnosing faults in electrical equipment. I can grasp a point quickly. I think I usually get my priorities right. And I know when I'm beaten."

"That last one is not necessarily a virtue."

"You think it's better to go on banging against a brick wall?"

"No, no. Of course not. One has to go on looking for the way over or round it, however hopeless it seems."

"Oh, I do that all right."

Peter took another sandwich and Dorothy picked up the little batch of handwritten sheets again. She had indeed, in this strange and unexpected moment of release, allowed herself to become a different person. Or rather, two different people. One part of her was feeling happier and more carefree than she had for years; the other part was terrified by the rate at which this unsought-for acquaintanceship seemed to be progressing. She had always been completely faithful to Gerry. The lovers he endowed her with existed in his imagination alone. There was no time for any such involvements in Dorothy's life. After the death of her daughter, Irene, she had deliberately taken on more and more commitments, and so had Gerry. Friendships had been allowed to drop, social life had dwindled to nothing. They drugged themselves with work, avoiding all close personal contacts, sharing the same roof and the same table and the same bedroom but still managing to avoid each other. The terrible gulf of secret guilt and suspicion lay between them and there was no crossing it. The struggles and sufferings of her patients' lives were an open file to Dorothy; but her own case history was locked away, deep in the memory, where it festered and never healed.

She could not unlock it. She could not cure herself, neither could she find the will to ask for help. Gerry alone held the key, but he would never release her. On the contrary, he turned it ever tighter, rejecting the few tentative efforts she had made to bridge the gulf and always forcing her back into herself.

The strain of their life had been very severe, but Dorothy was the stronger and Gerry had been the first to crack. Five years ago he had broken down completely and made the first suicide attempt. On that occasion Dorothy had been frightened enough to ask a colleague for help. Drugs and a spell in hospital had brought Gerry back to the outward

appearance of what he had been before. Since than Dorothy
had kept up with everybody the fiction that he was going to
get better; even with her father, who was nearer to her than
anybody else in the world.

It took every bit of her energies to do her job, cope with
Gerry, look after the house, and keep an eye on her father,
who was elderly and in poor health and lived alone. For a
man to awaken in Dorothy any personal interest he would
have to have exceptional charm: like Gerry as he had been
when she first knew him.

This man sitting by her now had no such charm. But he
had something that mattered a great deal more. He had
calmness and balance; in his presence one felt security and
peace.

"What I think you'll have to work at," she said, still
keeping her eyes on the papers, "is dressing up your reports
a little so that the statements don't look quite so bald. It's a
funny thing nowadays," she added thoughtfully. "People
are obsessed with taking off all their clothes or baring their
souls for everybody to see, but when it comes to language
they seem unable to endure the simple statement, naked and
unadorned.

"And yet we are supposed to be very permissive about
language," said Peter.

"Yes, but it runs alongside this frightful squeamishness
about making a simple statement. Read the sociologists or
economists. Listen to any current affairs radio discussions.
No one ever says 'yes' or 'no' or 'I don't know' or 'it might
be.' They say 'in point of actual fact we have to take into
consideration the undoubted possibility that in the eventual-
ity of . . .'"

"I can't write like that," said Peter.

"Heaven forbid that you should."

"But you said I ought to dress it up for the examiner."

"I shouldn't have used that phrase. I should have said
you could make some of the sentences sound less abrupt.
Here for instance."

Dorothy leaned forward to show him, but he got up and came to sit on the settee beside her and they looked at the exercise together.

"And here." Dorothy made a few more suggestions and then reached for a cigarette. The impulse to fling her arms around him was overwhelming. Just an ordinary uncomplicated person, she was thinking. I hardly ever meet any. It's wonderful. Like fresh bread and butter. "You have a go at the next paragraph," she said.

Peter did so, nervously at first but gaining confidence. Then he took out a pen and made a note of their redraft and compared it with his original.

"Well?" asked Dorothy.

"Yes. It's an improvement."

"Not dressing-up. Just a spot of polishing. For heaven's sake don't lose your capacity to go straight to the point. It's an invaluable asset. Incidentally, this recording-machine that you are recommending sounds a great improvement. I wonder if I could persuade them to buy one at the hospital for—" She broke off abruptly. The last thing she wanted was to give any hint of her own position.

"You work in a hospital?" said Peter with quick interest.

"Yes."

"Medical? Admin?"

"Yes," said Dorothy again.

"Yes which?"

"Ssh." She held up a hand. "I thought I could hear my husband calling. Excuse me."

This was not entirely an excuse for not replying to his question. She really had heard a faint sound coming from upstairs. She found Gerry awake and peering over the side of the bed.

"Dropped the stick," he said sleepily. "Wanted to bang on the floor for you."

"I heard it. Are you feeling better? D'you want anything to eat yet?" She was arranging the pillows again, quickly and efficiently. There was no more emotion in her voice than if Gerry had been a casualty patient. If he had not been so dopey he might have noticed this and resented it. As it was, he simply murmured that he would like a cup of tea.

"I'll get it," said Dorothy.

But when she was at the door he called her back, "Doll."

"Yes?"

"Thought I heard voices. Who is it?"

"The man's come to mend the washing-machine."

It was extraordinary that it could slip out so glibly while her heart was pounding so and that Gerry could accept it without question, sleepy as he was.

— 3 —

When Dorothy came downstairs she found that Peter had taken the tray out to the kitchen and washed up.

"Thanks," she said, suddenly feeling very embarrassed in his presence. "He wants some tea. I'll make some fresh. This is rather stewed."

Peter ran water into the electric kettle and plugged it in.

"Thanks," said Dorothy vaguely, longing now for the whole little incident to be at an end and yet dreading his departure. Open University student, she was saying to herself; electrician; came through the Hampstead Tutorial Service—there's enough information there to track him down again. But what excuse can I make for doing so? You're crazy, woman, she told herself in the same thought; your life is bad enough as it is. Don't make an even worse mess of it. Nip this nonsense in the bud at once.

"Having trouble?" Peter was looking at the washing-machine. There was a screwdriver and a hammer lying on top of it, left from Dorothy's hasty and unsuccessful attempt to get the lid to shut properly.

Dorothy nodded. "I meant to phone them about it but haven't had the time yet today."

15

"I'll fix it if I can. Don't worry," he added, instantly reading her mind. "I won't stay too long. You said you were free till quarter to four."

"Yes. I've got a—"

Again she pulled herself up. She had very nearly said "a patient coming." She began to laugh and Peter looked up at her enquiringly.

"My husband wanted to know who was downstairs," she said, "and I didn't want him worrying because he'd forgotten about a student coming, so I told a lie and said it was the man come to mend the washing-machine. It's rather disconcerting to find you've been speaking the truth when you intended a falsehood."

He made no reply and she was afraid that she had offended him by seeming to be putting him in his place as a tradesman. She went upstairs again wondering anxiously how she could put it right with him before he left. It would be unbearable not to part on the same terms of cheerful and equal fellowship that they had so miraculously achieved in this brief meeting.

Gerry was lying listening to the radio with his eyes closed when she came into the bedroom.

"Can you hold the cup?" she asked. "Or shall I hold it for you?"

He did not immediately respond and she knew with sickening certainty that he had detected something odd about her. His sensitivity to her slightest change of mood or feeling was uncanny. It's going to be hell, she thought; even worse than ever.

"Does your hand feel strong enough?" she asked patiently.

"To hold a teacup? Yes." He looked up at her for a moment and then shut his eyes again.

"I'm leaving it here then. Just by the radio. Don't knock it over. Are you sure you don't want anything to eat?"

"Later," he murmured. "Later. You're busy now. Men

mending washing-machines and patients and things. Busy, busy Dorothy.''

''All right then.'' The familiar helpless fury surged up in her again as she left the room, this time shutting the door behind her.

Her hands were still tightly clenched when she returned to the kitchen. Peter glanced at her curiously for a moment before returning to his work. A few minutes later he said, ''That ought to do if you give it a good bang. Don't let them try to sell you another. There's plenty of life in this yet. It's not a bad model.''

''Thanks,'' said Dorothy. ''I'm very grateful.''

She wanted to offer to pay for the work but knew that she must not, and she was relieved when he spoke.

''Exchange of services. A repair job for a tutorial. Okay?''

''Very much so. I've had the better bargain.''

''It's too early to tell. This may go wrong again tomorrow, but I've really learnt something from you. I wish you could take me on as a pupil. Would it be very unorthodox? Would your husband be very offended if you did?''

''It would be a bit difficult,'' said Dorothy, thinking hard after her first reaction of wild delight. ''You see, I'm out at work much of the time. This happened to be a free afternoon. And I'm not qualified to teach English, which my husband is. Very much so. He was head of the English department in a big school until he had a bad breakdown some time ago. That's why he's doing this tutorial work. It's keeping his hand in until he's fit to take on a heavy job again.''

''I see,'' said Peter, and again there was that curious glance, instantly withdrawn. ''It would be awkward if you were to steal his pupils. I don't think I'll trouble to ask them for another tutorial, though, if he really has forgotten about me, and I'll tell the agency I've changed my mind. You're quite right. I ought to make the best use of the Open

University facilities instead of getting in a panic and chasing after private tutors. But you've helped me a lot this afternoon and I'm very grateful. Goodbye."

And he held out his hand in the same abrupt manner as when he had first introduced himself. Dorothy took it and neither of them could let go. They made no further movement towards each other, but it was as if they were both clinging to a lifeline.

"I should like us to meet again, though," said Dorothy with the sensation that the line had given way and she was plunging down the edge of the ravine, "because I've not been quite honest with you."

"No, you haven't, have you? I have got a wife, by the way. You'll have been wondering about that. At the moment we are having a trial separation. She doesn't like me studying and I don't like her choice of companions. If she's as satisfied with the trial as I am, it will be made permanent. She's got our house at present and I'm living in a couple of rooms in Camden Town. You're welcome to pay me a visit if you like, but I must warn you that it's rather sordid. I'm sure you wouldn't mind that, but perhaps you'd like to make another suggestion, since I take it that it would be awkward for me to come here."

Dorothy managed to withdraw her hand at last. "Do you ever go for walks on the Heath?" she asked.

"I used to. There's not much time now between work and study, but I'll make it if you can."

"My father lives in a block of old people's flats near Parliament Hill. I always go and see him Tuesday evenings and I shall be there tomorrow. If I leave him a little earlier than usual, it will still be light enough for a stroll."

They fixed the exact time and place. If Peter suspected that Dorothy's father was to be used as an alibi for a longer than usual absence from home he did not say so. After he had gone, however, Dorothy became intensely conscious that this was her intention. I'll tell Dad I'm going early to meet a friend, she said to herself; he knows how impossible

Gerry makes it for me to bring anyone home. He can think I'm going to have a drink with Pauline.

But the thought of deceiving her father in this way worried her even more than the thought of keeping Peter's existence a secret from Gerry, and she stood still at the foot of the stairs for several minutes, holding her face in her hands and frowning.

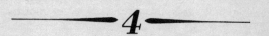

4

"You've not been listening to me, Doctor," said the plaintive elderly voice.

Dorothy controlled a start. This was only too true. Mrs. Bertram, the four o'clock patient, had been burbling away as usual and her own thoughts had been miles away. Desperately she tried to remember what had been the main theme of this session so far. The fear of cancer, which Mrs. Bertram did not suffer from. The arthritis, from which she did, but not very badly. Or the detested son-in-law with whom Dorothy had a sneaking sympathy, as she had with so many of the close friends and relatives of her patients. These were the three main struts that supported Mrs. Bertram's bored and idle life, and they occupied roughly equal parts in her thoughts. If she had been a poor widow instead of a rich one, her neighbours, or even her cat, would have been performing the service that Dorothy was now providing, and her chances of becoming less depressed and anxious would have been very much the same as they were with her present expensive treatment.

Such patients were unrewarding but they were often the only ones who could afford to pay, and Dorothy needed the money. For there was, of course, very little chance that Gerry would ever be able to resume his career. In fact, he had recently been talking of abandoning even that little effort of which he was capable, and Dorothy had an uneasy feeling that today was a turning point and that from now on he would never work again. He had a certain amount of insurance money and disability benefit and the house was his own, inherited from an uncle. But it was Dorothy's earnings that kept it goiñg, clothed and fed them, paid for the cars and enabled them to live as if two large salary cheques were coming along regularly every month.

Dorothy loved the house. Since the death of Irene it had been the chief consolation of her life and remained constantly in her mind and heart as something to work and plan for. If she bought a vase or a picture for the sitting-room it was as if she were choosing a gift for a lover or a child. She was ashamed of this passion of hers and afraid of it too because it made her so vulnerable. Nobody else knew how she felt. Only Gerry, who watched her and studied her and read her through and through. She would never be able to leave him because if she did she would lose the house. And she would never be able to leave him because she could not endure her feeling of guilt if she did.

Neither of these statements was ever uttered, but the truth of them both lay heavy between them in all their dealings with each other. Neither of these facts was ever forgotten.

It would be nice, thought Dorothy, to transfer Mrs. Bertram to a junior colleague of hers who also needed the money, and take on a patient who was more capable of making progress, but there was no question of it.

"I am listening, Mrs. Bertram," she said in the voice of quiet authority that patients found so soothing. "Please go on."

The next few words gave her the necessary cue, and after a little while she repeated her usual reassurances and mild exhortations. They came easily enough, through long practice, and as usual the old lady went away considerably comforted.

If only someone would do the same for me, thought
Dorothy as she took out the correspondence referring to the
next appointment. But it's only till tomorrow evening, she
told herself, and then I am going to tell Peter all about it. Or
at any rate, all about some of it. She stopped reading and
looked, unseeing, out of the window. It was she who was
mad, not Gerry. If she couldn't bear the pressures of her life
any longer then she ought to talk to someone at the hospital
about them. Or to her father. Or even to Mrs. Oliver, the
cleaner, who probably saw and suspected more than most
people because she came to the house every morning.

The trouble was that Dorothy had kept quiet about it all
for so long, had patched up Gerry again and again,
pretended to everyone that he was getting better. A
convalescent mental patient was best helped by being
treated like a normal person, not by emphasizing the
differences. That had been her guiding principle with Gerry:
to restore his self-esteem, his status in his own eyes and in
other people's. But she had carried it too far and persisted
with it long after she should have sought outside help. Not
only was there this terrible secret between them, but she had
also built up a barrier around them both that neither of them
could break through. They were imprisoned behind it,
destroying each other.

And now she was going to talk to a stranger because there
had been that extraordinary flash of recognition and understanding between them. She knew nothing about Peter but
what he had told her of himself, and that was not much. She
had noticed him looking with interest at her pictures and
china, and, for all she knew, he might be a would-be burglar
who had made up the story about wanting English tuition to
cover up an unsuccessful attempt to get into a house full of
valuable knick-knacks. Except that he had written that
exercise for discussion and he knew the name of Gerry and
of the tutorial agency, and it would be easy enough to check
with them or with the Open University people. It might be
sensible to do this. But she didn't feel like being sensible.
At the moment she didn't care if Peter Tarrant were a crook.

She believed he could help her and that was all that mattered.

She skimmed through the letter on the desk in front of her, replaced it in the folder and put it back in the drawer. It concerned another commonly-met-with type of patient. A sixteen-year-old girl referred as an emergency from a young people's rescue service. A child who had run away from home and was drifting about miserably from one group of communal-livers to another, hanging on to the edge of them, tolerated but not cared for, unable to settle anywhere or to make any permanent relationship of any kind. She had been picked up by the police after an eviction struggle and taken to the temporary refuge, where she had found a bottle containing a few sleeping tablets that someone had left lying about and had swallowed the lot.

As if I hadn't got enough of that already at home, thought Dorothy. But when the girl arrived she was more in control of herself than she had been with Mrs. Bertram and for the next forty-five minutes gave every bit of her mind to the frightened and hysterical child. Irene would have been about this age if she had lived, thought Dorothy. She always said this to herself when she met a girl of the approximate age group. These were the only times when she allowed herself any conscious recollection of the child who had died so long ago.

The case of Nina Farrell was probably a hopeless one. She was the offspring of a casual student affair, and her mother, disliking her from the first, had hung on to her in the hope of getting Nina's father to marry her. A sad old story. Nina's childhood had consisted mostly of waiting alone in the flat, hungry and frightened, for her mother to come home, and of being violently quarrelled over by her mother and her grandparents, who had refused to take her on themselves but would not stop interfering. Material conditions had improved when her mother eventually married a man much older than herself, but Nina was more unwanted than ever. She ran away from home a number of times, and on one occasion managed to track down her own

father, only to be rejected yet again with unnecessary
violence. She had no other relatives and no friends. There
seemed to be nothing good and positive in Nina's experience of life on which to build. She really needed to start her
life all over again and receive at least a modicum of love
and attention in some caring surroundings. And there were
so many like her. Dorothy was about to utter a few kindly
reassurances and tell her to come to the outpatient's
department at the hospital on Friday when she caught the
girl's eye and saw in it such an agony of pleading that her
heart contracted.

"If you will come along and see me here at the same time
next week," she said instead, "we'll be able to have
another talk about it and perhaps by then I'll have some
better suggestions about helping you."

"Are you sure you mean it?" The girl looked at her
suspiciously.

"Of course I do. Why should you think I don't?"

"Because most people don't."

"Well, I do. I want to see you again at five o'clock next
Monday afternoon, and I don't want any nonsense in the
meantime, Nina. No more drugs, and you are to stay in the
hostel. And give them a bit of a hand with looking after
the house. They could do with it."

"I'll make them a cake," said Nina unexpectedly.

"That's a good idea," said Dorothy, mildly amused and
hoping that the badly harassed warden would be co-
operative about this.

"I'll bring you one too, shall I?"

"Yes, please," said Dorothy.

Nina smiled suddenly, looking quite pretty in a pale and
waifish way. When she had come into the consulting-room
she had looked as if she would never smile again. I'm
breaking all the rules today, thought Dorothy after the girl
had gone. Letting sympathy run away with me and
becoming personally involved with a patient who will have
to be treated without payment. I wonder where it is all going
to end?

5

"I've sometimes wondered," said Peter, "what doctors and priests and others who carry other people's burdens do when they find they can no longer stand it."

"Well, now you know. They drag unfortunate technology students away from their studies and pour out the lot."

They were sitting on a bench at the edge of a clump of trees. In the distance was the vast pulsing, sprawling mass of London. A little way down the hill a few boys were kicking a ball about in a desultory manner. They had not, after all, walked very far. Dorothy's appearance had belied her statement that she was not too tired. Peter had said nothing, but as soon as they came to the bench he had said, "Let's stop and look at London a bit. This must be Dick Whittington's view."

"Just about," agreed Dorothy. "Are you ambitious, Peter?"

"Yes. I certainly don't want to be an electrician all my life any more than I wanted to be an unsuccessful farmer like my poor father. But we're not here to talk about me. Another time. You were going to tell me something about yourself."

She had told him then, without any effort and without any reserve, about Gerry's breakdown and the suicide attempts. That was half an hour ago and they were still sitting on the same seat.

"I'll have to be going soon," she said, "or Gerry will be getting suspicious and phoning my father."

Peter stood up. "We'll walk slowly back to the car," he said, "and talk on the way. Why did you marry him? No, that's a silly question. Why does anyone marry? I mean, did you not realize that he was terribly jealous and possessive when you married him? Or did you know it but think you could cope?"

"Both, I think," replied Dorothy thoughtfully. "And also . . ." She hesitated a moment and then laughed. "He's very good-looking. I was flattered that a man like that should take any notice of me. I didn't have many boyfriends when I was young. I was ugly and clever and emotional and intense. A ghastly combination, don't you think?"

Peter made no reply.

"What I like so much about you," said Dorothy, "is that you don't feel obliged to make some sort of feeble comment on what I've just said. If you've nothing to say, then you say nothing. It's wonderful."

"I should think you must get very tired of hearing people's voices in your job. It must be worse in a way than to be always looking at diseased bodies."

"I love my work," said Dorothy defensively. "I chose it."

"Look out." Peter caught her arm. They had come to a pathway and a boy on a bicycle was heading straight for Dorothy without looking where he was going. When he had passed they walked on together holding hands.

"I haven't felt like this for years," she said. "I feel about sixteen."

"And I feel rather ancient. It's a great responsibility, being confidant to an eminent psychiatrist. I'm not sure that I'm quite up to it, simple-minded mechanic that I am."

Dorothy glanced at him with a flash of anxiety, saw that

he was laughing at her, flung his arm backwards and forwards, and then let it go and ran ahead towards her car.

He caught her up and put a hand against the driver's door to prevent her from opening it.

"When are we meeting again? Or is this just a one-off job?"

"Ah, so you are human after all, Mr. Tarrant."

"I—" He drew a deep breath. "Now listen. You wanted to tell me and you feel better for doing so. Right? If that's all it's to be, just say so at once and I'll know where I am."

"What do you want it to be, Peter?"

"For the time being I'd just like to help you if I can. But not being a psychiatrist, I can't be detached about it. And your husband is obviously a very sick man and I don't somehow relish the thought of a regular discussion of all his symptoms, poor devil. But if that's the only way to help you, I suppose I shall have to stick it."

"Let's get into the car," said Dorothy. They did so, and then she said, "I wouldn't dream of inflicting it on you. As regards poor Gerry, this is definitely a one-off occasion. Just speaking it aloud has taken off the pressure. Now that I know somebody else knows, I'll be all right. Can't we meet again like this and talk about something else? Yourself if you want to. Or electrical engineering. Or music. Or dogs. Or cooking. Or absolutely anything you like. Oh, if you knew what heaven it is for me to talk to a really *sane* person!"

"So that's the attraction. I was rather wondering. I thought it couldn't be for my brains or my beauty. But, Dorothy, surely you do have some people in your life who are reasonably sane. Friends? Relations? People at work?"

"My hospital colleagues are mostly half-way bonkers themselves. It's an occupational disease among us. And friendship isn't easy to keep up in circumstances. It was my oldest friend Pauline who actually introduced me to Gerry in the first place. I think she'd got her eye on him for herself and was shattered when he started taking an interest in me."

"So you feel guilty about that too."

"Not exactly, because he wouldn't have married her even if it hadn't been for me. But it's a constraint between us. So we don't talk about him much if we meet."

"And relations?"

"There's no one close but my father. He's a retired clergyman. He's spent his life in tough parishes trying to sort out people's troubles. He's got emphysema and his heart's shaky and he's very tired and he's just had enough. He knows how ill Gerry has been, of course, so we can talk a little but I can't tell him the lot. I *can't*."

"Well, it's not my business," said Peter, "and of course I haven't met your father, but all the same it's hard to believe that he hasn't guessed. And if it's from him that you've inherited your character, then he'll be the sort of person who would want to know, however tired and ill he is."

"You may be right. I've told him about you, by the way. I hope you don't mind."

"Of course not," said Peter, but Dorothy, looking at him suddenly, thought he looked slightly taken aback.

"I didn't want to feel he was being used to cover up a secret assignation," she added rather self-consciously. "I said we'd met by chance and liked each other and wanted to continue the aquaintance. I said we were going for a walk on the Heath."

"What did he say?" asked Peter with unconcealed curiosity.

"He said he hoped we'd enjoy ourselves."

"That was all?"

"That was all."

"Most remarkable."

"Dad knows when to keep quiet," said Dorothy. "Like you. In fact you are rather alike. I wish you could meet him."

"Why not?" said Peter.

"It's taking up too much of your time. Unless," added Dorothy thoughtfully, "he could tutor you instead of Gerry. That's an idea."

Peter seemed to think well of it too.

"Do you know, I believe he'd enjoy having a little job like that," went on Dorothy. "And he'd be able to help you quite a bit. You'd have to watch him, though, and make sure he didn't get too breathless. Shall we meet an hour earlier next Tuesday and I'll take you to see him?"

The arrangement was made. Dorothy drove a little way and then said, "I suppose I'd better drop you here."

"Unless you want me to come and meet your husband too. I'm quite prepared to if it will make you feel any easier."

"I don't think it would," said Dorothy, thinking over the suggestion quite seriously. "He's fiendishly jealous of anybody I talk to. Including Dad. And our daily help. And my patients. Not to mention all those lovers that he's invented for me. I think it would be easier if he goes on imagining them and doesn't have an actual face to stick his stories to."

"You're sure he won't suspect my existence except as the man who came to mend the washing-machine?"

"Quite sure," said Dorothy firmly.

This was a lie. Dorothy knew perfectly well that Gerry had guessed that some sort of new influence had come into her life, subtly changing her own attitude towards him. Not only this, but Gerry probably knew the exact time when this had taken place. But if Peter thought he was putting her in some danger, or even making things more difficult for her with Gerry, then he would probably feel he ought quietly to slip out of her life. Such a prospect was unendurable.

Peter gave her a very keen look, as if he saw through her pretence, but to Dorothy's great relief he said no more. I don't really like deceiving him, she told herself; when we know each other better and I feel more sure of him I'll explain why I had to tell that lie. And perhaps one day I will be able to tell him about Irene too. But not yet. I can't bear to speak about it yet. Not even to Peter, who understands so well.

6

"How was your father?" asked Gerry glancing up from the crossword puzzle.

The radio was playing loudly and he did not trouble to turn it down as he spoke. He had been playing either the radio or the record-player more or less continuously ever since Dorothy had found him in the bathroom the previous day, and always the sort of music she disliked. In his saner and happier days he had disliked it himself. She didn't know now whether he used it as a sort of drug or whether he only did it to annoy her.

"Not too bad," she shouted through a particularly noisy patch. And then, in a blessed interval of comparative silence, she added, "I'm tired. I'm going to bed to read a bit."

She retreated towards the door of the sitting-room. The radio clicked off.

"Just a moment," said Gerry.

Dorothy turned at the door. His voice had sounded quite as usual and he was looking at her in what appeared to be a friendly enough manner. And yet it was at that very moment that she became conscious of the first icy shiver of a fear that was to become more and more intense.

"What is it, Gerry?" she asked, assuming a greater weariness than she actually felt. "Is anything the matter?"

"I've finished the crossword but for two clues," he replied in the most mundane of tones. "Perhaps you will have an inspiration."

And he read out the clues. Dorothy instantly supplied one of the solutions. The word was "murder." As soon as she had said it she felt that little shiver of fear again. She was quite sure from his reaction that he had already solved it for himself and was only asking her in order to make her repeat the word aloud. Every little thing that Gerry did or said had a hidden purpose behind it. Even when well he had had a tortuous mind that delighted in subtleties and undercurrents of meaning. And now his words and actions were more calculated than ever.

He had wanted her to say the word "murder." Was this some new sort of blackmail? A hint that he proposed to accuse her openly of murder or attempted murder? Or was it a warning that she might herself be in danger from him? The sickness of his mind had not, up till now, taken the form of violence towards her or to anybody except himself, but nothing was impossible with somebody in Gerry's condition. The one thing that was quite clear was that both she and Gerry had reached some kind of turning-point in their relationship with each other, and it certainly was not a turn for the better.

"What was the other clue again?" she asked, pretending to stifle a yawn.

Gerry read it out. "'Direction in hospital room gave notice.' Six letters, something A something N and if murder is right, it ends in a D."

"No idea," said Dorothy after a moment's pause.

"Pity, I thought you'd get it," said Gerry, staring at the newspaper. "Hospitals, you know."

"Sorry, can't help," said Dorothy abruptly and left the

room before he could speak to her again. The solution was "warned" of course, as he had obviously seen for himself, being a quick crossword-puzzle solver, but he was trying to get her to say this word too. "Murder" and "warned." What was she supposed to make of that? Was it intended as a serious threat towards her or towards somebody else? Or was it nothing more alarming than a new variation of his cat and mouse game with her?

Dorothy pretended to be asleep when Gerry came up to bed. She knew that he was no more taken in by this pretence than she had been over the crossword clues, but it was a relief all the same, because she felt less able than usual to cope with Gerry this evening. Confessing part of her troubles to Peter had greatly eased her mind, but oddly enough it had at the same time lowered her resistance to them. She had been stronger alone, with nerves stretched to the uttermost. The tautness was gone and there was no longer a risk that she might snap; but she felt weak and frightened in a way that was quite new to her. Suppose Gerry were to track Peter down and attack him? Or, even worse, suppose he were to get at Dorothy through her father? Peter was tough and could defend himself. Mr. Thorn was old and sick and vulnerable. Gerry's twisted mind would enjoy making Dorothy suffer through him.

And it would all be through her own fault.

Long after Gerry had fallen into a drugged sleep, Dorothy Laver lay awake with her mind chipping relentlessly away at the forms his madness might take. Her last waking thought was that nobody, not even herself in her professional capacity, had the power to force him to go into hospital care until after the damage had been done.

In fact, Dorothy was totally unprepared for the first manifestation of the change in Gerry. Two days after her talk with Peter on Hampstead Heath she returned late from the afternoon clinic to find Gerry very carefully and self-consciously dusting the blue and white plates that stood on the pine dresser in the sitting-room. He had never done this before, nor taken any part in the work of the household. Dorothy's first thought was that he was going to break some of the plates because she liked them. Accidentally, of course, because the self-inflicted wounds on his wrists were still bandaged and his movements were awkward.

But such little pinpricks were so much less bad than the evils that she had been imagining that her first reaction was one of relief.

"Hullo, darling," she said cheerfully. "Didn't Mrs. Oliver come today?"

Dorothy looked around her. The room with its mixture of Regency and cottage-kitchen effects, and the climbing plants showing through the open window, was her greatest joy in the house. Mrs. Oliver shared her pleasure in it. She was a middle-aged woman with an invalid husband and few pleasures in her life. She had worked for Dorothy for six years, and there was quite a strong bond between them, even though with Dorothy's hours of work they did not see very much of each other. Mrs. Oliver always arranged the cushions in the high-backed rocking-chair in a certain way and Dorothy saw instantly that this had not been done.

"Hasn't Mrs. Oliver been?" she asked again, and went on before Gerry could answer, "I do hope that doesn't mean her husband is worse."

"As far as I know," said Gerry, replacing a plate and standing back as if to check that it was in the right place, "there has been no change in the condition of that mysterious invalid husband of hers. We didn't even refer to him in our brief conversation this morning."

"Then what—" began Dorothy, but broke off abruptly.

Gerry had turned aside from the dresser and was standing behind the settee, resting both hands on the back and looking at her. He was smiling, but it was a travesty of the charming humorous smile that was one of the things that had first attracted her to him. It did not reach the eyes, and the look in the eyes was vicious.

This is another stage set for me, thought Dorothy, and the little lightning flashes of fear quickly came and went. I am intended to ask what has happened to Mrs. Oliver, she thought, and he will let it out slowly, drip by drip, dragging it out as long as possible.

I won't play his game, I won't ask, she said to herself. But instantly the thought came, If I frustrate him in this way, what will he do in revenge?

She decided to try to compromise, steeling herself against whatever unpleasantness she was going to hear.

"Oh well," she said in her brightest bedside manner, "I'm sure there's some very good reason for it all. Tell me about it over supper. I suppose there'll be nothing prepared, but we can have an omelette or get something from the freezer."

Dorothy was walking towards the kitchen as she spoke. She could better bear whatever revelations were to come if she was moving about busily rather than sitting or standing still.

"Such a busy little woman," said Gerry following her, and she knew from the spiteful tone of voice that he was very annoyed because things were not going according to plan. "Ever so sorry I can't be of more help to you," he continued, moving about the kitchen immediately behind her. "Oh—you want to use the bigger plates? I'm ever so sorry. Yes, it has cracked." He picked up a plate that he had dropped. "Irretrievably, I fear. What a clumsy person I am! I shall have to try hard to be more use to you in future, shan't I? Poor, poor Dorothy. Such a lot of work in this house. Much too much work for you. Much too big for us. I really think the time has come for us to look for a smaller house, don't you? Such a pity, after all the work you have put into it, and it is a credit to you, I must say, very unusual, very charming. Not exactly beautiful, but very striking. Striking and original, like Dorothy herself. Not to everyone's taste. But some people like it. I liked it myself. But it's too much work. Especially now. Yes, I really think we are going to have to relieve you of the work of this house."

Dorothy, vigorously beating eggs, did not pay too much attention to him. Threats about selling the house were nothing new. They had distressed her when they first started but she had grown fairly hardened to them. She could, as a last resort, call in the law to her aid, but on the whole she did not believe he would ever take any action about it, partly because he would then lose the satisfaction of threatening her and partly because she believed he was not capable of the sort of sustained effort required for carrying through a matter such as the sale of a house.

Gerry must have sensed that his words were not having the desired effect, because he changed tack.

"Such a clever little woman," he said as they sat down to eat at the kitchen table. "She can even cook quite a nice little meal. Wonderful woman, your wife, they say to me. Or they think it even if they don't say it. Wonderful how she copes with everything. Big house and garden, that useless husband of hers, and that job. Oh that terrible job! Just one long series of crazy people! However does she do it? And patients coming to the house too. And men who come to mend the washing-machine."

He stopped suddenly and allowed time for this last remark to sink in before he began to talk again, this time with an affectation of sympathy.

"Yes, that really was the last straw, wasn't it? Poor old Doll. Ruined your free afternoon. First of all you have to cope with me and then just as you are getting a bit of peace and quiet at last, damn it if the man doesn't come along to mend the washing-machine. By the way, that was pretty quick work on the part of the electricity people. Usually one waits weeks for a repair. But you'd only just phoned them. When did you actually phone them, Dolly?"

His voice was friendly, quiet, faintly puzzled. Only somebody who knew him very well indeed could have guessed at the deadly purpose behind it.

"Can't remember," replied Dorothy, inwardly shivering but outwardly as placid as he was. "Was it last Friday? Or Saturday morning? Or . . . no, wait a moment . . . didn't I get one of the girls in the office at the hospital to phone for me?"

"It can't have been Friday or Saturday," said Gerry, watching her slice through an apple before taking a bite out of it, "because it didn't go wrong until Sunday morning."

"Then I must have asked one of the girls." Dorothy took another bite. "These are quite nice," she said with her mouth full. "New Zealand, I think."

"Poor Dorothy." Gerry reached out to touch her hand as it lay on the table gripping the remains of the apple. Instantly she raised it to her lips and chewed at the apple core. "Poor old Doll. So much on your mind you can't possibly be expected to remember about a trivial little thing like a repair to a household gadget."

Dorothy picked up a knife and cut off a section of cheese. She didn't really want any but it steadied her nerves to keep doing something. If I can only go on eating until I know the worst, she was saying to herself, I may get through it. She was still quite in the dark about what Gerry was really driving at. It had seemed to be something connected with Mrs. Oliver, and Dorothy wished now that she had let it remain there, because whatever unpleasantness was brewing up for her in that connection, it could not be as bad as having him go on and on about the washing-machine. Had he actually telephoned to check up on her call and been told there was no record of it? She could get out of that, she supposed, by throwing the blame on the vast impersonal organization of the Electricity Board, but he would be constantly nagging about the bill and asking when they were going to make a charge for the work done.

Gerry always had made a great deal of fuss about checking the household bills, even before his breakdown. He loved to find mistakes and would not rest until they were put right. Useless to protest that she was paying the bills in any case, that she didn't care about a few pence one way or the other, and that if they were never sent a bill for the repair, why not just keep quiet and be grateful? Dorothy swallowed bread and cheese and knew with horrible certainty that the subject of the washing-machine repair was going to be brought up again and again at every meal time and at other times too; it would be worried at until her nerves were raw and she could not endure another second of it, and then dropped until the next time.

"You must be wondering," said Gerry, "why I am taking such an interest in the matter. The fact is that if we are to be without a cleaner then it seems only right and proper that whichever of us has more time should bear the brunt of the household duties."

"Without a cleaner," repeated Dorothy, shocked but at the same time relieved that it had come out at last. "Doesn't Mrs. Oliver want to come to us any more?"

"I dare say she does."

"Is her husband worse?"

"Not that I know of."

"But she's given notice?"

"Oh no, my dear. You've got it wrong." Gerry's voice was very sweet and patient. "She isn't leaving us. It is we who are sacking her."

7

Dorothy pushed back her chair, got to her feet, and shouted and swore at him, ignoring Gerry's little smile of triumph and not caring what she looked like or how upset she sounded.

"What did you tell her?" she asked when she had exhausted the first upsurge of fury, but instantly went on, "No, don't trouble to answer that. It will only be a lie. Oh, poor Mrs. Oliver! Why should she have to suffer for our miseries! You are a poisonous bastard, Gerry. There was no need to drag her in."

"My motives for dismissing Mrs. Oliver were three in number." Gerry stood up and ticked off the points on his fingers, as if he were addressing a room full of students. "One, to save money. Two, to give me something to do. Three, to have the house completely to ourselves. I will amplify these in turn. The two first are closely linked. Saving money will become even more necessary if, as I fear, it becomes impossible for me to continue with the tutorial work. But it will then be even more necessary for me to have some sort of occupation. What more suitable than that I should take over the household duties in place of

38

Mrs. Oliver? Killing two birds with one stone. I shall not, of course, perform them with her efficiency at first, but no doubt I shall improve with practice. The third motive is rather more complicated and requires a detailed exposition . . . where are you going?"

Dorothy had gone out into the hall and was rapidly turning over the pages of a little book that lay on the telephone table. "Mrs. Oliver's address," she muttered. "I'm sure I put it in the book. It's somewhere in Camden Town."

"Why this haste?" asked Gerry. "A little note thanking her for past services would, I agree, be appropriate during the course of the next few days, but—"

"Here it is." Dorothy tore a sheet off the telephone message pad and copied the address on to it. "I'm going round to see her at once. Poor Mrs. Oliver. She must be dreadfully upset."

Gerry followed her as she fetched her handbag from the sitting-room and took out the car keys, and then he accompanied her to the front door, talking all the time.

" 'Dreadfully upset' is a more apt description of yourself at this moment than of the worthy Mrs. Oliver. I do assure you, my dear Dorothy, that there is no need for this excessive concern on her behalf. She has been told very politely that we have no further need of her services and has been paid up to date with a little extra. She has, I imagine, some regrets but with her talents and the shortage of cleaning women she will have no difficulty in finding another job, and I find it hard to believe that she has not weathered far more serious catastrophes during the course of her life. It's perfectly absurd to rush off like this as if you have been summoned to a particularly agonizing deathbed. You really are making a fool of yourself, Dorothy."

They were at the front door. She pulled it open, slammed it behind her, and got into the car, which fortunately she had not yet put away in the garage. She was trembling so much that she could scarcely hold the steering-wheel, and in backing out into the road she scraped against a lamp-post and broke the glass on a rear light.

The little accident steadied her. We shall never hear the
end of that repair job either, she thought, although it's my
car and I'm paying for it and it's nothing whatever to do
with him. Half-way along Middle Lane she had to stop for a
moment to allow a car to straddle the roadway while making
a sharp turn into a drive. She knew the driver slightly and
they smiled and waved at each other. It was reassuring to
Dorothy, this little glimpse of a normal everyday world
outside the horror that her own home had become, and she
drove on more confidently.

Princes Street was undergoing a transformation. One side
had been demolished and blocks of council flats were going
up. The other side consisted of a Victorian terrace with the
houses at one end either boarded up or vandalized and those
at the other showing signs of human habitation. In this last
section Dorothy found the number she was seeking, walked
up the worn stone steps to what had once been quite an
elegant doorway, and lifted what had once been a beautiful
and unusual brass knocker. There appeared to be no bell in
working order.

While she waited, her present misery and fear became
mixed with a remoter, less intense kind of distress. She had
spent her childhood in gloomy, decaying areas of large
cities. Only in his last few years before retirement had her
father consented to move to a pleasanter suburban parish.
Dorothy's mother had been a social worker, equally dedi-
cated to the unfortunates of this world. Neither of them had
ever put any pressure on the child to follow in their
footsteps, but on the other hand, neither of them had ever
fully appreciated the extent of the conflict in their daughter's
mind between her deep compassion and longing to help on
the one hand, and her squeamishness and sheer physical
revulsion from the smell and sight of poverty on the other.

Princes Street brought back many memories. Dorothy
shut her eyes for a moment and had a vision of her own
lovely Hampstead home.

Except that it was not her own and never would be while

Gerry lived. Dorothy shook her head violently and gave a little cry as the overwhelming longing for Gerry's death assaulted her again and made her dizzy with its force.

"Dr. Laver! Who'd have thought . . . whatever is the matter? Come in and sit down. Come on in now."

Dorothy felt herself being guided through the doorway and towards a chair. She sank back and shut her eyes.

"I'm terribly sorry, Mrs. Oliver," she said a moment later. "I felt quite faint for a moment. I'll be all right now. What a thing to do—to turn up unexpectedly on your doorstep and go and collapse on you!"

She tried to smile, but the big, haggardly handsome woman standing in front of her did not respond in kind.

"You're ill, Doctor," she said, "and I'm not at all surprised. Working yourself to death. Now what can I get for you? I haven't any spirits in the house, only some sherry, but I can go out and get something if you like."

"Just some water, please," said Dorothy.

Mrs. Oliver fetched it and Dorothy took a small white tablet from her handbag and swallowed it.

"It's only a very mild tranquillizer," she said, smiling with more confidence this time. "If I'd had any sense I'd have taken it before. Then I wouldn't have given you such a fright. Have I come at a very bad moment, Mrs. Oliver? You weren't busy with your husband, were you?"

Mrs. Oliver reassured her. Fred had had one of his better days and had gone out for a stroll and a drink. She hadn't been doing anything in particular, was thinking of letting down the hem of an old summer dress, that was all.

"Why don't you go on with it," said Dorothy, "if you don't mind me sitting here a little to recover."

"I might as well, I suppose."

Mrs. Oliver found some scissors and began to cut away at the stitches round the hem. Dorothy watched her in silence for a moment or two. She had the impression that now the first shock of her own appearance was over, Mrs. Oliver was feeling rather awkward and glad of something to occupy her hands. The room was a curious mixture of a few old pieces of solid mahogany and of cheap new furniture already beginning to look shabby. The armchairs in which they sat had been savagely scratched by sharp claws.

"Where's Bella?" asked Dorothy. She and Mrs. Oliver had on several occasions chatted about the cat.

"Out in the yard," was the reply. "She'll be in presently."

Mrs. Oliver turned the dress round and proceeded to clip round the other side of the hem.

She's waiting for me to begin, thought Dorothy, and suddenly she wished with all her heart that she had never come. What Gerry had said was perfectly true. The job in Hampstead was a pleasant one for Mrs. Oliver, but there were plenty of others to be had. Dr. Laver was no doubt regarded with respect and possibly even a little affectionate concern, but Mrs. Oliver had her own life and her own problems, and Dorothy was only on the fringe of them. It was Dorothy's crisis, not Mrs. Oliver's, that had led to this untimely and increasingly embarrassing visit. There seemed to Dorothy to be only two courses of action open to her. She could pour out her troubles to Mrs. Oliver as she had done to Peter, and in that case she would no doubt receive a great deal of affectionate sympathy which would be very comforting. Or she could explain away her collapse as convincingly as she was able, and back up whatever story Gerry had told.

The trouble with the first alternative was that Mrs. Oliver could hardly be expected not to tell her husband about it, and he in turn would tell some of his cronies, and the thought of complete strangers discussing the miseries of Gerry and herself was intolerable to Dorothy, for Gerry's sake as well as for her own. Besides, as she had discovered after talking to Peter, this unloading of her burden seemed to weaken rather than to strengthen her; she seemed to be one of those rare people who disprove the rule that a trouble shared is a trouble halved.

On the other hand it was useless to pretend to Mrs. Oliver

that there was perfect harmony between Gerry and herself.
Mrs. Oliver had seen and heard too much.

Dorothy decided to plunge straight in without thinking
any more.

"I'm afraid we've got in a muddle," she said. "I don't
want you to stop working for us at all, and I was very upset
when my husband told me he'd told you not to come again.
I think he must have been worried by something I said about
having to cut down expenses, but, in fact I'd been thinking
about something quite different . . ."

Her voice trailed away. The trouble was that she had no
idea what Gerry had really said to Mrs. Oliver. The other
woman, understanding Dorothy's confusion, came to the
rescue.

"You're not to worry about it at all, Doctor," she said
warmly. "I quite understand. Truly I do. Mr. Laver was
very kind and explained it all. He said he wouldn't be able
to earn much for the next few months, but he did feel up to
doing the housework, so that it seemed only sensible for
him to do it and save my wages."

So Gerry was telling the truth about that, thought
Dorothy in a bemused manner. How clever of him, to do
something nasty that still enabled him to tell the truth.

"It does seem strange for a man to be looking after the
house," went on Mrs. Oliver. "I can't quite get used to it
myself, but after all, why not, as Fred always says. He's
quite happy to clean up when he's fit for it and get me a meal
ready for when I come in from work, so why shouldn't Mr.
Laver feel the same? That's what I said to myself, Doctor,
and although I've always liked coming to you, I quite
understand. So you're not to worry about it any more.
You've quite enough to worry about already. More than
enough in my opinion. No, you're not to rush away again—
not without a cup of tea. Not after having a turn like that.
You sit and rest yourself, and now you know you haven't to
worry about me you'll be feeling a little better. I'll soon
have it made."

And she left the room. Dorothy lay back and closed her eyes. One part of herself was deeply grateful to this nice, sensible, understanding woman for taking control of the situation and making it so easy for her. But the rest of her was panicking worse than ever. She felt as if a trap was closing round her, a trap set by Gerry. To have Mrs. Oliver coming regularly into her home had been a considerable source of comfort and support. And now it was to be removed. Gerry's unpredictable behaviour and her own reserve had driven away all the acquaintances who once used to call. Between them they had made it a very unhappy house to visit. No wonder people stayed away. And now the house was to lose its last little focus of steadiness and sanity. There would be nobody left to cross the threshold except a few patients—sick and self-centered people—and Gerry himself. Except for business callers such as the gasman coming to read the meter.

Or the man coming to mend the washing-machine.

Dorothy shifted in her chair and gave a little moan. She was going to have to do something about it. She could not live in that house alone with Gerry any longer. She was too afraid. But what to do? Even if she could bring herself to the point of just walking out on him, she would never dare to do it. Gerry could take too terrible a revenge.

Mrs. Oliver came back with the tea-tray. Dorothy sipped and made conversation about Fred and the cat and the present miserable condition of Princes Street.

"It'll be better when they've finished building the flats and got people in them," said Mrs. Oliver, "though I wish they didn't have to pull down all the old houses. I wish they'd just done them up a bit and put in bathrooms like they've been doing in Victoria Avenue."

"Victoria Avenue?" Dorothy's heart began to thump. This was Peter's address. "Is that far from here?"

"Just round the back," said Mrs. Oliver. "Same sort of houses, but some of them don't look at all bad now they're painted up. You get nice big rooms in these older houses—

gives you a bit of space to turn round in. Mind you, I wouldn't mind a nice modern kitchen."

Dorothy chatted a little longer, insisted on Mrs. Oliver accepting a ten-pound note as a goodbye present, and begged her to keep in touch.

"Let me know what sort of job you find and whether you are happy," she said.

"And you take care of yourself, Doctor. A good holiday, that's what you need. And Mr. Laver too."

"Perhaps I'll be able to persuade him to a week or two in the country," said Dorothy. "But he doesn't much like being away from home, you know."

They were standing in the shabby handsome entrance at the top of the broken steps, opposite the steel framework of the building site. A thunderstorm was brewing. The evening sky was lurid and oppressive. Dorothy felt an overwhelming sense of desolation, as if the last doorway that might lead to hope was being closed on her. She came down the steps and stood leaning against the dusty privet hedge that encircled the stone front yard. The car was only a few yards away, but for the moment her legs felt powerless to carry her so far. A sad little old man walked by, carrying a big load of washing for the laundrette. Then came two teenaged boys, one black and one white, moodily kicking a tin can along the gutter. A car and a post office van drove past, and after that there was no life in the street save for a black-and-white cat.

Dorothy bent down to stroke it, but it snarled at her and ran through the railings.

I wish I were dead, she said to herself, straightening up again and at last walking the few yards to the car. She got in and drove a little way, taking the first turning to the left and then the first left again, and drawing in to the kerb at the first vacant space. There was no road sign within view, but according to Mrs. Oliver's remarks, this must be Victoria Avenue. Dorothy was not conscious of any intention of seeking out Peter, or even of hoping that she might run into him by chance. In fact, she was conscious of nothing except extreme lethargy. The effort of shifting the car a hundred yards had totally exhausted her. I can't go any further. I'll just have to stay here, she said to herself.

She leant against the side of the car and shut her eyes. Her muscles felt paralysed but at the same time she was intensely conscious of every sound about her. This seemed to be a livelier road than the neighbouring Princes Street and quite a lot of traffic went by. There were also doors opening and footsteps passing and children crying and dogs barking. And after a little while came the first faint rumblings of thunder. When the crashes became very loud and the rain came down in sheets Dorothy opened her eyes. She had always enjoyed thunderstorms, and even in her present condition felt a flicker of the familiar sense of release that came from the lightning and the lashing of the rain.

When the worst of it was over she still felt deadly tired but no longer paralysed. She put the car into gear, eased it carefully out into the centre of the road, and drove slowly along, glancing at the houses with Mrs. Oliver's remarks in mind. One side of the road was very dilapidated, the other looked quite smart. Peter lived at sixty-eight. An even number. The shabby side. But she was not going to call on him, she told herself, and she drove on without glancing at the numbers on the door any more.

She had turned out of Victoria Avenue and was going past a row of shops, some of which were still open, when she saw him. He had his head bent against the still driving rain and was carrying a big blue plastic bag. A car moved off from the kerb and she was able to pull in. She leant across to wind down the window of the passenger seat and he looked up and saw her.

"Get in," she said. "I'll run you home."

"I'm absolutely soaking," he protested.

"It doesn't matter. The seat's wet anyway. I forgot to shut the window. Laundrette?" She watched him heave the bulging bag over to the back seat.

"Yes," said Peter. "It's not worth getting out the van to drive round. And I might as well have saved the money for the dryer. I ought to have waited till it stopped raining but I hadn't taken enough to read and was getting very bored. We'd better go round the block. You'll never do a U-turn here."

They drove round the block in silence.

"More trouble?" said Peter when they had stopped as near as it was possible to get to No. 68. "Were you coming to see me?"

"Oddly enough, I wasn't." Hastily Dorothy explained the situation about Mrs. Oliver and her own reactions to it. "It sounds idiotic," she said at last, "because it's not as if she is a close friend or anything, but it meant a lot to me, having a sensible person coming regularly to the house, and after I'd left her just now I really felt as if I only wanted to die. It was terrible. Everything seemed to be blocked in every direction. I've always believed I could understand how people felt in a suicidal state of depression. But I couldn't. It's much worse than I thought. And that was only a few minutes of it. I suppose Gerry feels like that most of the time."

"I don't think it will help you to try to imagine how Gerry feels," said Peter sharply. "I think you'd better stop that."

"I'm sorry," said Dorothy. "Was I getting hysterical? I'm very sorry." She swallowed convulsively. She was indeed very near to tears, and if they once started there would be no end to them.

"Were you proposing to go home now?" asked Peter.

"Yes. What else?"

"You could stay the night here if you like. I'll clear out and leave you, or stay and cosset you. Whichever you prefer."

"It would only be putting it off," said Dorothy doubtfully.

"True, but you might feel a little bit more able to cope with it in the morning."

"I might go home and find him really dead in the morning," she muttered.

"I was afraid you'd say that. So you want to go home now." It was more a statement than a question.

"Yes," whispered Dorothy, "but I don't know if I'll be able to manage if he's cut his wrists again. Or done anything else."

"In that case, we shall just have to send for another doctor, shan't we?"

"We?"

"I'm coming with you. Just let me dump this wet washing. Like to see my pad?"

"Yes," said Dorothy, wondering whether this was just his tactful way of ensuring that she did not run away while he was inside.

"Gosh, you really are organized!" she cried a moment later.

Peter had the two back rooms on the second floor. They were newly decorated and adequately furnished, but the most surprising thing about them was the big chart pinned on the wall of the bigger room. It was a timetable of his studies for the year, containing dates of radio and television programmes, tutorials and counselling sessions, together with numerous neat notes about books to consult, questions that needed revision or special attention, and various similar memoranda. On a large table was a tape-recorder, a radio, a pocket calculator, various types of graph paper and geometrical instruments, and a pile of books. Some sheets of paper covered with calculations and writing showed that he was at the moment struggling with some sort of exercise.

"How many hours a day do you work?" asked Dorothy after exclaiming again at this scene of industry.

"Eight at my job, four at my studies, which sometimes includes things like a couple of hours in the afternoon having a private English tutorial. Three hours spent travelling—mostly in traffic blocks. Two hours for eating and shopping and laundretting and suchlike. Seven to sleep.

That's my twenty-four. A very chaste and sober life." He made a face. "I only hope I can keep it up for long enough to get my degree."

"I can quite see that there's no room in it for a wife or even a mistress," said Dorothy. "And no room in it for wasting time with the likes of me. I'm going back home alone, Peter. I feel I can face it now. It's helped me no end, just having this glimpse of your tremendously orderly existence. Honestly it has. You don't know how much good it does me, just knowing you're there beavering away."

"Come on," said Peter. "I don't think we ought to delay any longer."

"But Peter . . ."

"Hurry up."

She protested all the way downstairs and out into the street. The rain had stopped and the evening felt fresh and clean.

"Are you feeling fit to drive?" he asked.

"Yes, but honestly—"

"Then you start off and I'll follow you in the van. When we get to Middle Lane I'll park on the other side of the road a little way back from your gate. Leave the gate open after you've driven through. If you find everything is all right, come out and shut it and that will be the signal for me to go away. But of course we won't speak to each other or make any contact. If you want me to come in, just stand at the gate and I'll come at once. If you don't appear within twenty minutes I shall come and investigate. Got that?"

"Yes. Thank you, Peter."

"I shall be anxious to hear how you are, though, even if you do come out and shut the gate. Can I phone you at the hospital tomorrow?"

"Yes, I'll probably have a patient with me, so I'm afraid I shall sound rather formal."

"That doesn't matter. As long as I know you're all right. Let's go."

8

It was just on ten o'clock when the blue Vauxhall turned into Middle Lane, followed at some distance by the little Ford van. The road was not very well lit, but the sky was by no means dark, and the white gateposts of Pond Cottage showed up clearly. Peter kept his eyes on them until he began to feel hypnotized. The minutes passed and Dorothy did not appear. At a quarter past ten Peter got out of the van and walked up and down the road, trying to appear to anyone who might see him as if he were taking a casual stroll, but in reality feeling more and more anxious every minute.

At nineteen minutes past ten he walked through the open gateway of Pond Cottage and up the drive. Light shone from every window of the house, as if a party were taking place there. It made the total silence seem all the more uncanny. If murder or attempted murder had been committed here, surely there would be some sign or sound or feel of it. Surely it would not be like this, just a blaze of light from all the uncurtained windows of a silent house.

Peter came up to the front door and stood close to it, listening intently. There was no sound to be heard from within. He turned the handle and gave a little push. The door was unlocked. He opened it very cautiously, keeping well behind it and being prepared to spring backwards any moment. Dorothy had been very much afraid, and fear was catching. For all he knew he might be walking into a trap. Suppose this husband of hers really was a maniac, homicidal as well as suicidal, and had knocked her unconscious and was now lying in wait for her supposed lover. It was perfectly idiotic, of course, but all the same he could not help his imagination running a little away with him.

Maybe Dorothy herself had set a trap for him. After all, he knew nothing about her except what he could see for himself: that she was fascinating and very attractive in an odd sort of way; that she was under great stress and very much afraid. If what she had said of her husband was true, then he certainly ought to be in some sort of care other than that of his wife. But Peter had never even seen the man and all he knew of him was what Dorothy herself had told him. Could it all be a complete fabrication? Would it not be possible for an overworked psychiatrist herself to have some sort of mental breakdown that led her to imagine herself threatened and to invent fantastic stories? Or if it was true that her husband was making her life a hell but that she could see no way to free herself, then wouldn't she be longing for somebody else to free her?

Peter was almost sure that Dorothy was absolutely straight and really was going to the utmost lengths not to drag other people into her own troubles, but he could not quite suppress a little nagging doubt.

What he saw next increased it.

Since the front door seemed to be free of booby traps, and nobody appeared to be lurking behind it, he stepped into the hall. At the same moment Dorothy appeared from the kitchen at the back of the house. She did not immediately see him and he caught the expression on her face before she had brought it under control. It was a blood-chilling mixture of hatred and horror. Her mouth was slightly open, her teeth clenched; her skin was dead white and her violet eyes looked as black as her hair.

She saw him and the muscles relaxed, and she once more looked intensely weary and anxious but quite sane.

"Is it time already?" she asked. "I thought there was another minute to go."

"It seemed a long time," he replied. "I was getting very impatient."

"I'm sorry. He's not here, but I didn't want to call you until I'd made quite sure that he wasn't in the house."

"You're sure now?"

"More or less. I've looked everywhere. Cupboards and all."

That explains the lights on in every room, thought Peter. She left them on as she went round. She really is in a very bad way.

"Would you like me to come round with you to look again?" he asked.

"I don't think it's necessary. Thanks all the same. He left a note, you see. But I didn't trust it. That's why I was checking."

Her voice was dull and lifeless. She shut her eyes and seemed to sway a little. Peter caught her arm.

"Come and sit down and tell me."

In the sitting-room he turned out all the lights except one reading lamp. Dorothy leant back on the settee.

"I found it in his study," she said. "I went there first. If he doesn't answer when I come in, it usually means I'm going to find a message there. This was a longer one than usual and rather different." Her voice shook and she took several deep breaths before going on. "I told you what it usually is," she continued. "Self-reproaches. Wants to end it all in order to stop being a burden to me. I always destroy them immediately. There weren't any self-reproaches this time. It was all directed against me. He's going to kill himself in order to—in order to—"

Again she had to pause and take a deep breath. "In revenge for an injury that I once did him. He threatens to kill himself in such a way that it will look as if I have murdered him. That's what he says. He doesn't say how or when or whether it's going to happen in this house or somewhere else. That's why I felt I had to go all round the house before I called you. He might have been lurking somewhere and I'd have been dragging you into a trap."

"I see," said Peter. "May I see the letter?"

"I'd rather you didn't. It seems . . . it seems treacherous to him somehow." ●

"Treacherous! And you've been subjected to a threat like that! I'm all for loyalty and for standing up for people and covering up their weaknesses, but to carry it to these lengths . . . it's insane."

"Yes, I think perhaps I am a little mad myself," she said wearily. "It's probably just because I hate him so much that I feel I've got to protect him and that I can't stand anyone, even you, to see his outpourings. Least of all you."

Peter did not ask why. "Listen," he said patiently, "I'm not asking to see this letter because I want to feel superior to your husband or because I have any pleasure in reading such things. I'm only asking so that I can try to form an opinion for myself of how serious the threat is and what we ought to do about it. You'll say I can't judge because I know nothing about mentally ill people. I say you can't judge because you're too emotionally involved. But between us we might manage to make some sort of objective assessments. Is that sense or isn't it?"

Without a word Dorothy fished in the pocket of the short raincoat that she was still wearing and drew out a few folded sheets of paper. Peter read in silence. He tried to prevent an expression of distaste from forming itself upon his face but was not sure that he had succeeded. The contents of the letter were exactly as Dorothy had said, much embroidered with abuse and interwoven with descriptions of her relationship with her "lover." Whether it was more revolting than it was horrifying Peter could not tell. Certainly it aroused both sensations, but also, in spite of it all, one could not help but feel pity for the man who had written it.

Dorothy's circumstances and Dorothy's feelings became very plain to Peter as he read her husband's letter. And yet the little niggling doubt about her remained and was reinforced when he asked the inevitable question.

"This last sentence—I don't get what he's referring to."

Gerry had written: "You really would like to die, wouldn't you, Dolly, so that you can stop feeling guilty about Irene."

"Who is Irene?" asked Peter.

"That's the—the reference to the injury he thinks I did him," said Dorothy.

Peter made no comment on this evasive answer, but simply handed back the folded sheets of paper and said, "I think we ought to call the police."

"Oh no!" It was a cry of horror, much as he had expected.

"It contains a threat that has to be taken seriously," went on Peter solidly. "A double threat. Against himself and against you."

"I can't, I can't." Dorothy became very agitated. "That would mean everything coming out. It'll all be churned over again and again, and we'll end up in exactly the same position as before. There's nothing on earth that anyone can do so long as it's all threats and no action."

"But there has been action. He's made lots of suicide attempts. You said so."

"Only token attempts. It used to be a crime, but it isn't now."

"Then what happens if somebody finds an attempted suicide and reports it? Surely they are taken to hospital? Surely they are?" persisted Peter as Dorothy did not immediately reply.

"Yes, if they need treatment," she said at last.

"And what then?"

"They pump out the stomach if it's poisoning or do whatever else is needed. Then they discharge them."

"Oh come now, Dorothy! I know we're short of mental nurses and doctors and hospital beds, but surely they don't just shove people back into whatever situation drove them to try to kill themselves without making any attempt to find out what's the matter and give them some help?"

"A quarter of an hour in outpatients once a month. Once a week if you're lucky." Dorothy's laugh held a ring of hysteria. "Not exactly adequate for delving into the depths of a human soul and trying to put it in order. That's a twenty-four-hour-a-day job, you know."

"I see," said Peter soberly. "I hadn't realized the situation was as desperate as that."

"It is very desperate. Mental illness is the epidemic of our era. People like me can do no more than put a finger in the dike to hold back the flood."

"But surely in your position . . . you would have some pull when it comes to your own husband . . ."

"Get him into a hospital psychiatric department ahead of the queue, you mean? Certainly I could do that. There're only two objections. First of all, there's practically nothing they can do for him except give him the sort of pills he's having already. Secondly, he wouldn't stay. He's not certifiable, you know. You have to do quite a lot to be that. And with anyone other than me he sounds quite rational and plausible. He happens to have an excellent intellect. He'd make rings round any doctor who tried to prove him *non compos mentis.*"

"I'm sorry," said Peter. "I'm afraid I hadn't fully realized the position. All right then. We don't ring the police. We just wait on events. Is that what you suggest?"

"For tonight, at any rate," said Dorothy. Her little burst of spirit had spent itself and she sounded dull with weariness again. "And since he may come back at any moment, I think you'd better go, Peter. It won't help if he finds you here."

"I'm not leaving you alone."

They wrangled about this for a minute or two.

"Then I'll call somebody else to stay with you," he said eventually. "Somebody above suspicion. What about that friend of yours. Pauline, was it?"

"Oh no!" Dorothy shrank from the idea. "I can't possibly tell Pauline. She married somebody else and is a widow now, but I believe she's never really stopped being in love with Gerry. We only keep friendly by not talking about things."

"Then I'll phone your father. Now shut up. So he's old and tired and has a tough life behind him. What sort of a life are you having at the moment? How do you think he would feel if anything frightful were to happen to you and he hadn't even been given the chance to prevent it? Come on. What's his name? What's his number?"

Dorothy supplied them. Peter dialled the number.

"Mr. Thorn? I'm sorry to be ringing so late . . . I hope you hadn't gone to bed . . . Good . . . My name is Peter Tarrant and I know your daughter—I believe she's mentioned me to you . . . Yes, I'm here with her at her home and she's in a spot of trouble . . . no, she's not ill, she's perfectly all right. It's about her husband. He's disappeared. Gone off and she doesn't know where. I don't think she ought to be alone here in case there's some bad news . . . oh good, I hoped you'd say that. I'll come and fetch you . . . fifteen minutes or so—traffic's not so bad this time of night . . . thanks very much. We'll be there." He put down the receiver. "Come on. I'm not leaving you alone here, even for half an hour."

Another wrangle began. Before it had got very far the telephone rang. Dorothy lifted the receiver.

"Is that you, dear?" said her father's voice. "Is Mr. Tarrant still there?"

"Yes," said Dorothy.

"Then keep him there. I'm getting a taxi. Shan't be long."

And he rang off before she had a chance to reply.

Peter laughed when Dorothy told him. "I'm going to like your father," he said. "He obviously knows just how to deal with you."

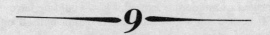

9

The Reverend William Thorn turned out to be almost disconcertingly like Dorothy in appearance, except that the thick hair was shining white instead of black and the eyes were faded violet. He was tall and upright and had the same way of holding his head. Faintly aloof, unconsciously arrogant, Peter told himself. A man who did not bend or break easily, probably a man who did not find it too easy to establish superficial relationships with people, but who seemed to have an outsize conscience, like his daughter.

"I quite agree that we don't want to do anything that might make it harder for Gerry to get over this," he said when the situation had been explained to him.

Peter noticed that Mr. Thorn did not appear either shocked or surprised when told about the numerous suicide attempts. It was evident that he had guessed that something of the sort had been going on, and Dorothy's protectiveness, as Peter had himself suspected, had been to a large extent unnecessary.

"I'd like to see this last letter of Gerry's, please," said Mr. Thorn.

"It's rather beastly, Dad," said Dorothy.

"Is it? I dare say I've seen worse at one time or another."

Reluctantly Dorothy handed the letter over and Mr. Thron read it without comment. Then he folded it up neatly and put it in his pocket. "I'd better keep it safe," he said. "If anything has happened to Gerry it will be needed as evidence."

How well he knows her, thought Peter again; she would destroy it if she got half a chance, even though it might be vital for her own protection if indeed Gerry had carried out his threat to kill himself in such a way that she would be suspected of murdering him. But how could he have done so? If he had got a gun and gone and shot himself on the middle of Hampstead Heath, Dorothy would no doubt blame herself for it, but there would have to be some very solid evidence for Dorothy to be suspected of murder.

Peter spoke this thought aloud. Mr. Thorn was inclined to agree that Gerry was still alive. But where? "I suppose you made sure he wasn't in the garage," he said.

Peter shook his head, annoyed with himself for not thinking of this obvious precaution.

"The car," cried Dorothy. "That must be it. We've got two Vauxhalls. Same model. Keys fit them both. Oh, what a fool I am!" She clenched her hands and banged at the sides of her head. "It's obvious. He's gassed himself from the exhaust and rigged it up to look as if I've done it."

"How?" asked Peter bluntly.

"How do I know how?" Her voice rose. "He's so bloody clever he'd fix it somehow."

"But why," asked Peter in the same down to earth way, "should he go to all that trouble to throw suspicion on you and then ruin it all by writing his confession in that letter?"

"Because he's mad. That's why."

"Wouldn't we have heard the engine running if that's what he'd done?" persisted Peter.

"Not necessarily. The garage is round the side. The doors will be shut. We were very preoccupied."

She spoke in a jerky, breathless manner. Her hands were twisting together and there was a hint of that look in her eyes that Peter had seen when he came upon her unawares. His doubts returned, not in a little niggling way, but with a sharp stab. She could have been pretending all along, he thought; twenty minutes is quite a long time. And I wasn't watching the house and garden, only the gateway. I saw nothing but the gateposts.

Suppose after she found the letter—that's genuine surely—she searched everywhere and found him in the garage. Unconscious or semi-conscious. As on earlier occasions. Found him in time to bring him round. Again as on earlier occasions. And decided not to. Perhaps even hurried it on. Perhaps he'd left himself enough air to survive and she closed the opening to make sure. Then she'd have come to the gate and told me everything was all right. But she was too late. I came a minute too early. She couldn't get rid of me. She had to change her plans. I don't blame her. I only wish she'd been honest with me.

He stared at Dorothy and she stared back.

"Don't you think we ought to go and see?" said Mr. Thorn, beginning to get up from his chair.

Dorothy jumped up and pushed him back. "Not you, Dad. You oughtn't to be involved in this at all, in your condition. I'll go myself."

"No," said Peter reaching the door of the sitting-room before her. "I think it would be best if I go."

Again they stared at each other: their eyes were very nearly on a level.

"Very well," said Dorothy. "You'll need the spare key to the garage. He may have locked himself in. It's an ordinary wooden door like a shed. The old coachhouse."

She went into her consulting-room and came back with a key.

"Do you always keep it in there?" he asked.

"Yes." She was very abrupt.

But she was coming from the kitchen when I came in and saw her, thought Peter. Does that mean she really doesn't know what's happened? Or had she already replaced the spare key in the consulting-room?"

"Thanks," he said. "I won't be long."

At the front door she called after him. "Don't try to move him if he's there. Call me at once."

"Yes, Doctor," he said and ran off round the drive to the side of the house.

Dorothy returned to the sitting-room and began to fuss over her father. "I do wish you hadn't been dragged into this. Are you feeling all right, Dad? I hope you hadn't gone to bed when we phoned."

"No, my love, I had not gone to bed," replied Mr. Thorn patiently. "I don't need much sleep and I never go to bed till after midnight. And I am feeling perfectly all right. I will tell you at once if I'm not. I wish you had been equally honest with me, Dorothy. It is very grievous to learn that Gerry has been behaving in this way and that you've kept it all to yourself. I suppose he has been tormenting you by making you feel guilty about the child, which is all nonsense. You know that, don't you, Dorothy?"

"Please, Dad. Please don't talk about her."

The pain in his daughter's voice was more than Mr. Thorn could bear to hear. "Well, there's no sense in wasting our breath on recriminations," he said. "We'll just have to carry on from here. I like your Mr. Tarrant. Economical sort of person. Very self-controlled. Doesn't waste words or effort. But not without feeling. I hope he's not going to be any the worse for this little adventure."

"I know I oughtn't to have dragged him in," cried Dorothy, "but he insisted on coming."

"Just as I did. Well, we shall know the worst in a minute or two. Poor Gerry. What misery he causes. A most unhappy soul."

Mr. Thorn shut his eyes and took slow, controlled breaths, conserving his limited energies for whatever shock was to come. Dorothy paced about the room, clenching and unclenching her hands.

"What was that?" she cried suddenly, standing still just inside the window and peering out into the garden.

Mr. Thorn stirred and opened his eyes but did not speak.

"I thought I heard voices." Dorothy left the window and came to sit on the arm of her father's chair. "I don't know how to bear it if he isn't dead," she said quietly. And then she clutched his arm. "Is that dreadfully wicked of me? Am I so very bad?"

"No, my love. Not bad." He soothed her. "Just terribly overstrained. But it's coming to an end now. It will soon be over. Do you understand that, Dorothy? We shall know in a minute what has happened. But whether Gerry is dead or alive doesn't matter. As far as you are concerned it is finished. Just hold on to that. In one way or another this is going to end. I promise you, Dorothy."

"Thank you," she murmured. "I'm sorry, Dad. I ought to have told you about it ages ago."

"Yes. Never mind. It's nearly over now. Ssh. Listen. Can that be Gerry?"

Mr. Thorn raised his head. The distant voices that Dorothy had heard sounded much nearer. There was a loud shout and then something that sounded more like an animal growl than a human voice.

"He'll kill him!" screamed Dorothy and ran out of the room and out of the house.

Mr. Thorn gave a helpless little shrug and leaned back resignedly. If he tried to intervene it might bring on an attack and he would be more nuisance than help; Dorothy would have two patients to look after instead of one. There was nothing he could do, but the minutes of waiting seemed very long.

The shouting died away. Mr. Thorn, listening intently, heard two voices coming nearer. One of them was Dorothy's; the man's voice was not so clear and it was not until they were actually in the house that Mr. Thorn could make out who it belonged to. He got carefully to his feet and walked towards the sitting-room door. The waiting had become intolerable.

"Mind his head," he heard Dorothy say, and then the

man's voice said, "All right. I can take most of the weight now."

The voice was that of Peter Tarrant, not his son-in-law. Mr. Thorn was conscious of a great sense of relief which he did not care to analyse too closely.

"In here," said Dorothy.

Mr. Thorn stepped back into the room and rearranged the cushions on the settee.

"Thanks," said Dorothy as she and Peter eased Gerry's limp body into a comfortable position.

Mr. Thorn bent over it. "He's not dead," he murmured.

"No," said Dorothy, "nor even fatally injured. You were wrong in thinking it's all coming to an end."

And she gave a hysterical laugh.

"I said in one way or another," said her father. His glance moved from her to Peter Tarrant. "Good God, man!" he cried in quite a different sort of voice. "Are you badly hurt?"

There was blood running down one side of Peter's face. Some of it had dripped on to the collar of his jacket.

"I don't think it's much," he said, putting a hand up to his forehead. "I'll see to it in a moment. Is there anything more I can do, Dorothy?"

Dorothy was standing completely still, looking down on her husband's unconscious body. "No, thanks," she said. "It's too late. It's a pity you didn't finish the job off properly while you were about it."

Peter's eye caught Mr. Thorn's and signalled an appeal.

"Dorothy," said the old man sharply, "you have two men here who need your skilled help. Are you going to give it to them or shall I telephone for an ambulance?"

"I'm sorry." Dorothy gave herself a little shake. "Come up to the bathroom and I'll clean up that cut," she said to Peter. "There's no hurry about Gerry. He won't come round just yet."

10

"He came at me when I was shutting the door of the garage," said Peter about a quarter of an hour later. "I can't remember exactly what he said. "Stop thief," was the gist of it. I said something like, "Are you Mr. Laver? Your wife's looking for you." And he said something more and then I noticed he'd got something in his hand. It looked like a breadknife. I got hold of his arm and managed to turn it round and to duck at the same time, and he caught me with the blunt edge of the knife. Surprisingly hard."

Dorothy gave a little shudder.

"Yes. Lucky," said Peter. "It's a beautifully sharp knife. I didn't fancy any more of that, and I hit him on the jaw. He went backwards and unluckily caught his head on that stone you've got for propping open the garage door. That's the point when Dorothy appeared on the scene." Peter turned to Mr. Thorn. "And the rest you know."

"But where had he come from? How long had he been there?" Dorothy looked at Peter. "Why didn't you notice him when you were watching the house? You could see the front drive." She sounded reproachful rather than mystified.

"I couldn't see round to the garage," he retorted. "Why didn't you look in the garden yourself when you were hunting for him?"

"I did look. All round the back. I couldn't find him."

"Then you must have been playing hide and seek with each other. In and out the bushes. Very charming."

"If you think I knew he was there all along and was setting a trap for you hoping he'd go for you and you'd kill him—" began Dorothy furiously.

"Dorothy, my dear," interposed her father.

"No, no. Let her go on," said Peter. "It's about time we got this straight. You accused me just now of not finishing the job properly."

"I was hysterical." Dorothy's fury subsided as quickly as it had flared up.

"Were you hysterical when I came into the house after waiting as we had arranged? You were coming out of the kitchen. You didn't see me for a moment. I was quite frightened by the way you looked."

"I'd had a shock," muttered Dorothy. "That letter."

"Yes. You'd found that letter at least fifteen minutes earlier. I think it was something else. Something you'd only that minute discovered."

"Don't you think, Mr. Tarrant . . ." began Mr. Thorn in quiet protest.

"I've got to know,' insisted Peter. "I'm in this business up to the hilt, whether I want to be or not. I could have lost my life over it. I don't mind taking risks and I'm not complaining. I want to help Dorothy if I can. But I don't want to be tricked into anything. I'd rather she didn't keep things so much to herself."

"Yes, yes. You've got a point," murmured Dorothy's father in some distress.

"While we were talking about Gerry poisoning himself with the exhaust fumes," said Peter addressing himself to Mr. Thorn, "I couldn't help wondering whether Dorothy hadn't already found him in the garage while she was alone here and had decided to let him finish the job, leaving it for me to discover the corpse because it would look better. We were to be kept talking here for long enough to let him die. I've no idea how long it takes for a man to kill himself that way, but I expect Dorothy knows."

He stopped and looked keenly at Dorothy. She was curled up on the settee. They had carried Gerry on to the couch in the consulting-room, put him to bed there, and left the doors open just in case there should be any sound of returning consciousness. There was nothing much to be done for him yet, Dorothy said. The concussion was probably quite severe but there was no open wound. When he came round it would be a matter of painkillers and sedatives.

"If Gerry jumped out on you from the bushes, then I couldn't have left him dying in the garage, could I?" said Dorothy.

"No indeed. It couldn't have been that that was worrying you when I came in."

Dorothy did not immediately respond. Her fingers pulled at a button on the back of the settee that was slightly loose, worried at it until it came away.

"Damn," she said. "It's awfully hard to find someone to mend these button backs." And then she continued, almost in the same breath, "You're right, Peter, I was practically hysterical when you came into the house and it wasn't just because of the letter. It's odd that you haven't guessed why. I should have thought it was obvious. I'd just found that the breadknife was missing."

Peter and Mr. Thorn looked at each other.

"We might indeed have guessed," said Dorothy's father. "And we might also wonder why Peter was not warned that Gerry was in possession of so lethal a weapon when he went off to look for him just now."

"D'you think I'm not blaming myself?" cried Dorothy passionately, getting up from the settee and starting her pacing again. "I don't know why I didn't warn Peter. I suppose I just took it for granted that Gerry was going to injure himself and nobody else. I just didn't think of mentioning it, that's all."

"That sounds so feeble that I think it must be true," said Peter.

"It is true! It sounds crazy, but it's true. It's not the first time Gerry's used a knife. It just never occurred to me that he might use it on anyone but himself. And I really thought he might have rigged up something with the car. It's not the first time he's tried two things together either. He once had an electric heater in a bath full of water and had just swallowed half a dozen tablets when I found him."

"Is the inquisition over now?" enquired Mr. Thorn, trying to lighten the atmosphere. "If so, then I think it's time we all tried to get some rest."

"I'll take you home, Dad," said Dorothy, very contrite. "Or would you rather sleep here tonight?"

"I would most certainly rather sleep here. I wouldn't dream of leaving you. But how about yourself?"

"Oh, I'll doze down here and keep an eye on Gerry," said Dorothy.

"That's not good enough," said Mr. Thorn, and Peter said almost simultaneously, "Can't you get a nurse in from an agency?"

"What am I to tell her if I do?" countered Dorothy. "That my husband has been in a fight? Don't you think it's best to keep the whole wretched business to ourselves?"

"I wish we could," said her father, "but I don't quite see how. Strictly speaking, we ought to have informed the police that an assault has been committed. Mr. Tarrant has legitimate cause to bring a case. Perhaps he would like to do so. Perhaps he thinks that would be the best way of helping you in the long run, Dorothy, disagreeable as it would be. Am I right, Mr. Tarrant? You have been considering it?"

Peter admitted that he had. "That's why I wanted to be quite clear about Dorothy's position," he added. "I didn't want there to be any danger of her being suspected of anything at all, and I don't see why she should be, in view of all the previous suicide attempts which will obviously have to come out. But it'll be a horrible strain for Dorothy, and it's not worth it unless it achieves its aim. Which is to get Gerry locked up and in proper care.''

"Would it do that?" enquired Mr. Thorn of his daughter.

"It might. For about three months,' said Dorothy bitterly. "And what then? But it's more likely that Gerry will win everyone's sympathy because of his unfaithful wife. Naturally he attacked his wife's lover. Who wouldn't? Naturally he often felt suicidal, knowing his wife was deceiving him . . . oh, what's the use of talking about it! It's hopeless. There's no way out. I shall just have to go on as before. I'm sorry I dragged you into it at all. Both of you. That must be Gerry.'' She cocked her head on one side and listened. "He's coming round. I'll have to go.''

After she had left the room Peter stood up. "I suppose I'd better go too. Unless you think there's any point in my remaining here.''

"At the moment, no," said Mr. Thorn. "We'd all better simmer down, I think. It's never wise to start discussing the possible long-term effect just after a crisis. But one always does it. I think I'll be able to persuade her to get him into hospital to recover from the concussion, at any rate, and that will give us a breathing space. Leave me a phone number where I can reach you.''

Peter wrote out a number.

"Thank you," said Mr. Thorn. "And thank you for everything else." He took the younger man's hand. "I hope that cut won't trouble you for long. You've been a good friend to Dorothy. And to me. I'm grateful.''

Peter pressed the old man's hand gently and noticed again the extraordinary resemblance between father and daughter. Intensity, vitality—a similarity of character, not of outward appearance alone. It was all the more remarkable in the father because of his physical frailty. He made Peter think of a powerful engine that might easily shatter the feeble framework in which it was encased, if it weren't for the strength of mind and will controlling the engine to ensure that it did not run too fast.

"I hope we shall meet again in any case," he said. "I'm very glad that you are staying here with Dorothy."

"Here I am and here I shall remain. If she tries to send me home, it will bring on one of my attacks of breathlessness. That will settle the matter. Gerry is not the only one who can work that ploy."

Peter laughed. "Good luck. She's got her match in you. I love her, you know, Mr. Thorn," he added conversationally, "but God knows what will become of it. Good night."

11

"Well, my love. You've news, I see."

Mr. Thorn was seated in a long garden chair on the lawn in front of Pond Cottage, half in and half out of the shade cast by the copper beech tree. It was Sunday afternoon. Gerry had been in hospital for three and a half days, during which time Dorothy had gone to work and seen a few patients at home, and Mr. Thorn had done a little shopping and cooking, a fair amount of sitting in the garden and reading, and a very great deal of thinking. In the evenings they had watched television or listened to records. Very little had been said about either Gerry or Peter.

By Sunday morning Dorothy had begun to look more rested, physically at any rate. But now, on her return from visiting Gerry in hospital, she had about her that haunted look again. She plumped down on the grass beside her father's chair and leant against his knee.

"He's much better," she said in a low voice. "They want to discharge him on Wednesday."

Mr. Thorn took a few of his carefully controlled breaths before he replied. "That'll be just a week. A week's not a bad breathing space. You're much better than you were."

"Yes," agreed Dorothy, and fell silent, plucking at blades of grass.

"Do you want to tell me about him?"

"There's not much to tell really. He's still very weak and seems rather dazed. Can't remember anything about how it happened. Or at any rate he pretends not to be able to remember. Very convenient, concussion. You can forget or remember just as you please. Gerry's going to make full use of it."

"It's convenient for you too," said Mr. Thorn after a moment's thought. "You don't want anybody to know that Gerry went for Peter with a knife, and you don't want anyone to know that Peter knocked him out. Now whatever Gerry remembers, or decides to remember, nobody is going to believe it on his evidence alone."

"Oh, he won't make any fuss publicly," cried Dorothy. "That's never been his way. He's always put on a beautiful public show. Even during his breakdown. He specializes in private emotional blackmail. And that's going to be worse than ever."

"Different, perhaps. Not worse. Don't forget that I'm living here now. The presence of a third person will rather cramp his style."

Dorothy twisted round to look up at her father's face. "You can't stay here after Gerry comes home," she said. "I can't bear it. I won't have him tormenting you too."

"Are you afraid he is going to go for me with a knife?"

"No. I don't think he will attack you. But he might attack me."

"In that case I shall call the police."

"I don't think he's going to attack me physically," said Dorothy. "He'll find other ways of getting at me. You can guess. I don't need to tell you. Please, Dad, I'm sure it will be worse if you stay here."

"I'm not going to leave you, so there's no point in saying any more. I am not afraid of a poor, sick, unbalanced mind.

It's no good arguing, Dorothy. I am not to be shifted and that's an end to it."

"An end to it! There's no end to it! And you promised me there would be, didn't you? And for a moment I believed you. Like a child. Never mind, darling." She got up from the ground. "It was lovely to be soothed and pretended to, just for once. Let's have some tea."

"I promise you again," said Mr. Thorn, rising slowly from his chair, "that this situation is not going to continue for very much longer."

"Really? How is it to be stopped? Either Gerry or I must die. That's the only way out. He'll never leave me, and I can't leave him. And he seems to be very good at not dying, in spite of everything. Perhaps I'd make a better job at suicide myself. I might well come to it. Is that what you were thinking of, Dad?"

And she pressed his arm affectionately, to show that she knew it wasn't, and to show that she was grateful to him for letting her talk and relieve her hopelessness in this manner.

"Think over what I suggested," said Mr. Thorn presently, "about getting some resident domestic help. I'll meet half the cost. The more people you have here as buffers between Gerry and yourself, the better. I would suggest an attractive au pair girl. That might cheer me up too. Italian preferably. Limpid and languorous. None of your big beefy blondes."

"You're a wicked old sinner, Dad," said Dorothy. "And it wouldn't work, you know. Gerry would never make love to her. I only wish he would. He'd nag her and make sarcastic remarks and drive the poor girl away."

"Then I would bring her back again. Think it over, Dorothy. Naturally whoever we get would have to be warned of his condition. That would be only fair. But some people would not mind. There's safety in numbers, you know. I'm a great believer in throwing in more and more factors when you've got what looks to be a hopeless situation. Stir it up a bit. Muddy the waters. When they clear again they could show quite a different pattern."

"Yes, an even worse one," said Dorothy, laughing. "A glamorous Italian girl with a knife in her throat and Gerry swearing I did it out of jealousy. That's what you'd call stirring it up, I suppose."

"Perhaps it will work the other way around. Perhaps the girl will murder him."

"No such luck." Suddenly Dorothy dropped her bantering manner and spoke in a muffled voice as she buried her head against her father's shoulder. "If only I could just be sorry for him. If only we could talk about it and comfort each other . . . or if only we could really forget it . . . Oh God, if only I didn't hate him so!"

"Suppose," said Mr. Thorn presently, "that a patient of yours was in the same position that you are, and asked your advice. What would you tell them to do?"

"I'd tell them not to give in to emotional blackmail."

"Well, then."

"It's different when it's yourself. If I walk out on Gerry and he kills himself . . . or if he carries out his threat and starts telling people about Irene . . ."

"Telling them what, my love?" asked Mr. Thorn after waiting in vain for Dorothy to continue. "What is there to tell? You lost your baby daughter. By a tragic accident. How can Gerry hurt you any more over it than you have been hurt already?"

Very gently Mr. Thorn tried to turn Dorothy's face towards his own, but she pulled away.

"I'm talking nonsense, Dad. I'm sorry. Don't let's talk about Gerry any more. It only makes me feel feeble and sorry for myself."

"Very well," said Mr. Thorn, and he did not mention Gerry again that evening, but he was more thoughtful than ever.

When Dorothy had left for the hospital the following

morning, Mr. Thorn dialled the number that Peter had given him.

"Is there any chance of your getting up to Hampstead this morning to look at the 'fridge?" he asked. "It's very awkward to have it not functioning in this weather."

"I'll try to get round between eleven and twelve," was Peter's reply.

"That will do fine."

Peter replaced the receiver. His friend and employer, Len Hardy, looking up from a complicated tax form over which he was frowning, asked, "New customer?"

"Could be."

"Big stuff? Or little nusiance jobs?"

"Too early to tell yet. I can fit it in on the way to the Healthfield Road job. See you, Len."

When Peter got to Pond Cottage, Mr. Thorn had some iced drinks ready.

"The 'fridge has miraculously righted itself," he said. "I hope you didn't mind my employing that little subterfuge."

"I don't much like telling lies to Len, but I suppose I must put up with it," replied Peter. "We usually tell each other about our friends and activities, but of course I haven't said a word about Dorothy."

"It's difficult for you, I know," said Mr. Thorn sympathetically, "but it would have been worse if I'd tried to tell you over the phone. Gerry is coming home on Wednesday."

"So soon? Surely Dorothy is in a position to—"

"Pull strings? I'm sure she is, but she won't. Her argument is that it would only be postponing the inevitable and that Gerry might be easier to handle if he doesn't suspect he's being kept in hospital longer than he need be."

"There's something in that, I suppose," said Peter, staring gloomily at his tumbler. "How is she?"

"A lot better than when you last saw her."

"Is she going to do anything about him? Other than just grin and bear it, I mean."

"I'm afraid not. I'm trying to think of minor ways to make her life more tolerable. I've a feeling she might agree to some sort of resident domestic help."

"That's a good idea," said Peter. "Somebody like Mrs. Oliver. She was frightfully upset about losing her. The more normal people she has about her the better she'll be. Look, Mr. Thorn—"

"Bill, please."

"Look, Bill, I know you'll be honest with me. Is there anything at all that I can do for Dorothy now? Or would it be better for her if I just slide out of her life completely?"

"My honest answer is that I simply don't know. I think it's probably better for you to keep away from the house for the time being. Gerry seems to have forgotten whom he hit or who hit him, but I don't think a meeting between you two would be very pleasant."

"But does she want to see me at all?"

"I don't know that either." Mr. Thorn looked at the strained and anxious face opposite to him and relented. "I don't know it for certain, but it's my guess that she does."

Peter did not look much happier. "I don't want to carry on an affair with another man's wife, whether he's a schizophrenic or not. Though if he were a normal person, it would be easier. But as it is, she's never going to leave him, is she?"

Mr. Thorn did not answer this question, but asked another instead. "You want to get on in life, don't you, and your studies mean a lot to you?" Peter nodded without speaking. "Dorothy was telling me you are doing an Open University degree," went on Mr. Thorn. "It takes great strength of purpose to stick to the sort of programme you've set yourself. I hope you won't think I'm being patronizing when I say I admire it enormously. And so does Dorothy. It would be a tragedy if anything were to happen to make you give it all up. Especially after the sacrifices you've already made."

"She's told you about Stella then," and Peter, looking

away. "It wasn't a bad marriage. She was inclined to think me dull, which I am, and I was inclined to think her silly, but we rubbed along quite well until I started getting what she called big ideas. She couldn't bear to sit quiet while I was studying, and I grudged all the time spent going to the pub. We had a few frightful rows and then decided to part company for the rest of the year and see how we both felt after that."

"Sad, but probably inevitable in the circumstances, and certainly very sensibly dealt with," said Mr. Thorn. "Do I take it that it's unlikely you will ever come together again?"

"Very unlikely. I ran into her the other evening with her current boy-friend. They seemed to be very happy and well suited. We'll probably get divorced in the New Year."

"So that's one problem solved," said Mr. Thorn. "I wish Dorothy's troubles could be so easily dealt with, but I'm afraid they look like taking up a great deal of time with very little result. They are emotionally exhausting not only to herself but also to everyone connected with her. You can't spare that time and that emotion, can you, Peter, if you're to fulfil your ambitions?"

"Why don't you ask me straight out if I'd be willing to give up my studies and my future if I could have Dorothy?" Peter's tones were aggressive.

"That was to be my next question," said Mr. Thorn, unmoved. "Let me phrase it another way. Suppose Dorothy were to agree to leave Gerry. Would you be willing to give up your plans in order—say—to emigrate to Australia and start again from scratch?"

"Of course I would! As if there'd be any question of it!" Peter stared angrily at Mr. Thorn.

"H'm. I see." Mr. Thorn stroked his chin. "But you wouldn't give it up for your wife?"

"That was quite different. You can't compare Dorothy with Stella."

"Dorothy has many faults, you know," said Mr. Thorn.

"Of course she has. Who hasn't? What does it matter?"

Peter was sitting back listlessly now. "I haven't a hope in any case, Gerry or no Gerry. Oh, she might fancy me for a little while. I think she probably does. But she'd never marry me. Dr. Laver, consultant psychiatrist, and P. Tarrant, electrician. Can you see it? Sounds daft, doesn't it?"

"I don't see anything the matter with it," said Mr. Thorn sharply. "You disappoint me, young man. I didn't expect this stupid sort of self-deprecation from you."

"Sorry." Peter got to his feet. "But I can see it's hopeless. All the same, I'd like to know what happens to her. And if she really would like to see me . . ."

He left the sentence unfinished.

"We know where to find you," said Dorothy's father. "I promise you won't be left in the dark."

12

"Goodbye, Mrs. Bertram," said Dorothy. "I hope you'll soon be feeling better."

"Goodbye, Doctor."

Dorothy stood at the window of the consulting-room and watched the small figure move slowly down the drive to where her daughter was waiting with the car. Mrs. Bertram was wearing a very elegant blue silk summer coat and hat to match, and the car that her daughter was driving was a Bentley, but nevertheless there was something pathetic and forlorn about the old woman. What's the point of it all, if that's how one ends up, thought Dorothy. But at least that was the last patient of the day, and she could look forward to a quiet evening with her father.

Then she suddenly remembered that she had told that little runaway girl to come again. Nina Farrell. Another hopeless case. Would she turn up? Most probably not. The girl would never stick out the week in the hostel. She'd probably drifted half across London by this time. Or been picked up by the police. Or drowned herself. There was no possible way in which Nina Farrell could be salvaged. On the whole Dorothy hoped she would not come. Her own

vitality was at such a low ebb that she had none to spare for
giving hope to hopeless cases. She frowned when she saw
the girl opening the gate, but irritation gave way to curiosity
as she watched Nina come up the drive.

The girl was wearing the same jeans and tunic, but they
didn't look quite so dirty, and she had washed and brushed
her hair. She was walking slowly and carrying with great
care what appeared to be some sort of square box. She
looked up at the house and Dorothy hastily moved away
from the window. The bell rang and Mr. Thorn, who was
coming into the hall at that moment, answered it. Dorothy
remained behind the slightly open door of the consulting-
room, curious to hear what sort of encounter there would be
between her father and Nina.

"Good afternoon," she heard her father say. "What can I
do for you?"

"Is Dr. Laver in?" asked the girl. The voice, too,
sounded stronger and rather more determined than Dorothy
had remembered it.

"Is she expecting you?" countered Mr. Thorn.

He's trying to protect me, thought Dorothy with affectionate amusement. He doesn't know she's a patient, and he
doesn't know what to make of her.

It was at that moment that the crazy idea first shot into her
head.

"Yes, she is," said Nina firmly. And then added, with the
anxious note back in her voice, "At least she told me to
come."

Dorothy reached for the door handle: it was time to
intervene. But she paused again when she heard her father's
next words.

"What have you got in that box? A hamster?"

"A hamster!" Nina was shrill with indignation, and
indeed Mr. Thorn had sounded rather as if he were
humouring a child. "It's a cake for Dr. Laver," Nina went
on. "I promised to make her one."

So she did, thought Dorothy with a little click of the

memory. How extraordinary! And what a long time ago it seems.

"Hullo, Nina," she said, coming out into the hall. "This is my father, Mr. Thorn. Miss Nina Farrell. Is that for me?" She relieved the girl of the big cake-tin and Nina and Mr. Thorn shook hands.

"What sort is it?" asked Dorothy, pulling at the lid of the tin. "Coffee icing and walnuts. Super. Look."

Mr. Thorn examined the cake. "A thoroughly professional job," he said. "It also happens to be my favourite. There's going to be some rivalry for the lion's share of that."

"You take it," said Dorothy handing him the tin, "and we'll all have a slice in a minute or two. I want to talk to Nina for a little while first."

"Yes, ma'am." Mr. Thorn made a little bow. "My daughter's the boss here, you see," he said to Nina, who looked at him uncertainly, not knowing whether she was meant to laugh or not.

"Well, Nina, how have you been?" asked Dorothy, motioning the girl to an armchair and sitting down herself in the chair by the desk. "Have a cigarette?"

It was very unprofessional to welcome a patient in this way, as if she were a visitor to the family, but Dorothy had her own reasons for breaking all the rules.

Nina, it seemed, had not had too bad a week at all. Dorothy, as she listened, wished she could say the same. The trouble was, apparently, to find somewhere more permanent to live. They couldn't keep her any longer at the hostel because there were so many emergencies, worse than she was, to take in.

"What were you thinking of doing?" asked Dorothy.

"I don't know. Go back to a squat, I suppose." Nina did not sound very enthusiastic at the prospect.

"Have you thought of trying to get a domestic job? You're obviously a good cook."

"I like cooking," Nina admitted cautiously.

"But not cleaning? Dusting and washing up and things like that?"

"Not very much."

"I don't suppose anyone does. But it has to be done. Could you bear it, do you think, and could you bear living in a dull and quiet household with only middle-aged people?"

"I don't know," said the girl. "I've never tried."

"No. Of course you haven't. Silly question. I'd better say straight out what I was thinking. My husband is coming out of hospital in a couple of days' time. My father whom you met just now isn't very strong. I have a full-time job and no help in the house. The cooking and shopping are the most important. We'd all help with the cleaning. There's a fair-sized sunny room on the top floor. You could have that and do what you liked with it. Fifteen pounds a week and all your food. It probably won't come to more than four or five hours' work a day, but it's got to be the hours when we need you. Otherwise your time is free. Well? What about it, Nina?"

Dorothy had been watching the girl closely while she spoke. After the first blank astonishment there had been some signs of anxiety, followed by the familiar suspicious look. At the mention of cooking, however, a gleam of enthusiasm had come into the girl's eyes.

"I can do Chinese dishes," she said when Dorothy had finished. "We had a chef in one of the squats and he showed me how."

"I like Chinese food, and so does my husband, but my father would probably rather have scrambled eggs. Does that mean you'd like to come, Nina?"

Nina opened her eyes very wide. "D'you mean it? You don't really mean it, do you? Come here and live with *you?*"

"Is it so very awful a prospect?" Dorothy tried to speak lightly. The expression on the girl's face was quite frightening. "Of course I mean it, Nina," she said, hoping to ward off a violent outburst of emotion. "I meant it when I told you to come and see me again, didn't I? It can't be a permanent solution, but it would help us both out for the time being. You need a home and I need someone to cook. I couldn't give you any formal treatment, but you could talk to me whenever you like, and we would look around for a suitable job or training for you."

The attempt to stem the threatened flood was unsuccessful. Dorothy gave a little cry as the girl flung herself upon her, clamped her arms around her neck, and cried as noisily as an infant in a tantrum. Dorothy's own arms tightened involuntarily about her and for a moment they clung to each other.

"There, that's enough," said Dorothy, shaken and appalled by her own reaction to the girl's passion of gratitude and hope. She disengaged herself gently. "How about that cake? My father will be longing to try it, but he won't start till we come."

After supper that evening, when Nina had gone off to fetch her few belongings, Dorothy and her father stared at each other.

"Don't say it," she begged. "It's too late. I can't let her down now. It was a sudden mad impulse, and I just gave way to it."

"I was joking, of course," said Mr. Thorn rather stiffly, "about the glamorous au pair girl."

"I know you were."

"What I had in mind was a mature student working her way. Preferably somebody with nursing experience. Someone who would be a genuinely stabilizing influence in the house."

"I know you did. It would have been a very good idea. Instead of which I take in a terribly disturbed child who's attempted sucide herself and is now clinging to me like a limpet because I stand for the mother who rejected her. And I'm clinging to her because . . ." Dorothy did not finish the sentence. She got up and came over to kiss her father. "I'm barmy, I know I am," she said. "But it's partly your fault. First of all you brought me up to have a social conscience and secondly you said that it was a good idea to add a new factor when you'd got a seemingly insoluble problem. What's worrying me at the moment is that I didn't tell her about Gerry. I just said he was coming out of hospital."

"It wouldn't make any difference if you'd told her there were ten homicidal maniacs living in the attic. She'd still want to come. You're going to have that girl with you for a very long time, Dorothy. And she's a lot younger than Gerry."

"Oh well, at least she can cook. I had my suspicions about the cake, you know, but she certainly did make that risotto herself. It was delicious, wasn't it?"

Mr. Thorn admitted that it was. Then he rubbed a hand over his eyes and said, "I think I really must be getting old. Somehow I don't feel I want to hear any more about the problems of social misfits and suchlike."

"Well, you can always go back to your flat, can't you?" said Dorothy mischievously. "I'm not keeping you here against your will."

Mr. Thorn opened one eye. "And miss all the drama? No, no. I'm seeing it through. What are Nina and Gerry going to make of each other. That's what I want to know."

13

The crucial first meeting between Gerry Laver and Nina Farrell, rival claimants for Dorothy Laver's sole attention and care, could hardly have taken place in a less auspicious manner.

Dorothy had arranged with the authorities in the hospital to which Gerry had been admitted that she would collect him herself at five o'clock and drive him home. On the way she would gently break to him the news about her father and Nina being in the house. But whether through some administrative muddle, or whether through Gerry's own machinations, he came out several hours earlier and took a taxi to Pond Cottage.

Nina and Mr. Thorn had had lunch together and had shared a huge bowl of strawberries and cream, for which both of them had a great weakness. Conversation had consisted of information about the lives of late-twentieth-century squatters, supplied by Nina, and about the lives of early-twentieth-century unemployed labourers, supplied by Mr. Thorn. Each listened with genuine interest to what the other had to say. Nina and Mr. Thorn, after an initial slight awkwardness with each other, were now getting on very well indeed. They had washed up together and then Mr. Thorn had gone for his usual little after-lunch stroll. Nina said she was going up to her room to get on with painting the woodwork her favourite shade of dark purple, but after the old man had gone she went back to the kitchen and took a big recipe book down from the shelf. She was thinking of making something very special for the homecoming of the husband of her beloved Dr. Laver and was glad to have the house to herself to cogitate about it in peace.

She sat cross-legged on the kitchen floor—a habit that was proving rather hard to break—opened the book at a luscious-looking coloured illustration, placed it on the floor in front of her, and then put her elbows on her knees and her chin in her hands and stared at the picture, deep in contemplation.

"Peppers," she murmured to herself. "There's two left. Paprika. Cream—I've some left over. Mushrooms—have we got any mushrooms?"

She got up and inspected the vegetable rack and then returned to her devotions. For what was possibly the first time in her life Nina Farrell was utterly absorbed and utterly happy.

When she heard the sound of the key in the front door Nina did not stir. The old man can't have gone very far, she said to herself, and thought no more of the matter. Then suddenly she raised her eyes from the book on the floor, pushed the hair back from her ears, and listened with her head tilted to one side, as alert and suspicious as a little wild animal. There was something about the sounds of movement going on in the hall that told Nina at once that this was not Mr. Thorn returning from his walk. When the old man came into the house he always rubbed each shoe three times on the doormat, wet or fine. Nina was very quick to recognize little habits like this, and after barely a couple of days in their company, she had already noticed quite a lot of such little mannerisms in both Dorothy Laver and her father. When she particularly disliked somebody she would mimic these little habits, and she was quite a good mimic.

But she had not the slightest desire to imitate either Dorothy Laver or William Thorn in any unkind way.

There was no sound of the scraping of shoes on the mat. Instead there were footsteps that sounded rather impatient and a strange male voice muttered, "Where the hell has she got to?"

Nina's head shrank down deeper between her shoulders and her apprehensive look intensified. In the kitchen doorway stood a tall man of about forty wearing a light lounge suit. He had a fine, Byronic-type head with thick brown hair, hazel eyes, and strong regular features except for the mouth, which was too small and had a petulant twist to it. It was turned up now, in what looked like a sneer, as he said in what Nina mentally described as a mean and uptight sort of voice, "And who might you be?"

"I'm Nina," she replied, and her own voice came out as a nervous squeak.

"Nina," repeated Gerry Laver. "Very brief. Very much to the point. But not particularly informative. What might you be doing here?"

"I'm the cook."

Nina scrambled to her feet with some idea of feeling less at a disadvantage if she were standing up, but it was not much help because her head only came up to Gerry's shoulder. Gerry looked her up and down with what his pupils, during his schoolmastering years, had called the lingering Laver look. It had a remarkable capacity for making its object feel thoroughly contemptible in every way. Gerry at the height of his powers had been quite well liked by his colleagues because he kept order in class, was reliable and hardworking, and punctilious about administrative detail. But his pupils, although they learnt well and usually passed their exams, had hated and feared him.

Nina, subjected to this merciless scrutiny, went crimson and looked around like a hunted animal seeking a way to escape.

"I see. You are the cook. We appear to be making some progress," said Gerry. "There are two aspects of your statement that puzzle me. My concept of a cook as a woman of a certain maturity and dignity is no doubt completely outmoded, but even in this enlightened era I confess I should have expected some lingering traces of those old-fashioned qualities. However. The second aspect is at the moment causing me rather greater concern. I appreciate that my memory is bound to be rather unreliable as far as the events of my accident are concerned, but external evidence tells me that I have been absent from home for barely a week. I am almost sure that my household did not boast the services of a cook, nor, to my knowledge, was there any intention on the part of myself or my wife to seek such services. But it seems that I am mistaken. In which case the concussion from which I have been suffering must have been more severe than I have been led to believe. I find this rather disturbing. Do please try to stand still for a moment," he concluded irritably, "and kindly enlighten me about your presence in my house."

Nina, who had been fidgeting about and twitching her face and hands all the time Gerry had been speaking, held on to the side of the kitchen table and made a great effort to control herself.

"I came to see Dr. Laver for treatment," she managed to say at last. "I needed somewhere to live and she needed help in the house and I can cook quite well so she offered me the job."

"I see," said Gerry. "Very interesting. Occupational therapy for a mental patient in the practitioner's own home. No doubt Dr. Laver proposed it as some sort of scientific experiment."

It looked for a moment as if he were about to embark on another long speech, but to Nina's immense relief he turned and left the room, only to return a moment later to say in a very offhand manner, "Presumably Dr. Laver will be home later and will fill in the necessary details herself. Meanwhile I am going up to my room to lie down and I should like some tea and biscuits brought up at half past four. I take it that is within the scope of your duties in my house?"

And he was gone before Nina had a chance to reply. A few moments later she heard the slight sound of a door opening and shutting on the floor above.

Nina let go of the kitchen table and slid down on to the floor beside the open cookbook. There she lay drumming on the tiles with her toes, banging with her fists, and whimpering and moaning uncontrollably.

Mr. Thorn, coming in a few minutes later, heard sounds coming from the direction of the kitchen and went to investigate.

"Nina! My dear child! Whatever is the matter?"

Nina continued to writhe and moan.

Slowly and deliberately, conserving his strength and making sure he did not strain himself, Mr. Thorn lowered himself on to his knees beside her, caught one of the flailing hands between his own and held it gently.

"You must get up, my dear," he said, "and come and tell me about it in the sitting-room. I cannot kneel like this any longer. I must sit down and rest."

Nina stopped shuddering, rolled over, sat up, and turned on the old man a face so twisted and smeared with tears and fury that it was barely recognizable.

Mr. Thorn got carefully to his feet. "Come on. Let's hear about it," he said.

In the blue-and-white room he settled himself comfortably and told Nina to shut the door.

"Now," he said, "what's happened to upset you like this?"

"He's come home too early," replied Nina, standing stiff and straight just inside the door and putting a deep tragic note into her voice. Then she came forward and beat upon the back of the settee with both hands and let out a stream of abuse against Gerry. It stopped as suddenly as it had begun and she put a finger to her mouth and bit on it and said, "I'd forgotten you were a clergyman. I'm sorry."

"Whatever does that matter?" said Mr. Thorn impatiently, and added, half to himself, "This is most unfortunate. Very unfortunate indeed."

"You mean you don't mind me swearing?" Nina looked at him wide-eyed.

"I dare say you had provocation. But on the other hand it must have been quite a shock to Mr. Laver to come home and find a strange girl in the kitchen. And people aren't exactly at their best when they've just come out of a hospital and when they've had concussion. And quite apart from that, Mr. Laver had a bad nervous breakdown not so very long ago. That also tends to make people rather difficult to get on with sometimes."

Nina sat down to listen to him and did not interrupt, but she looked very unconvinced at this defence of Gerry.

"You must remember that he is a sick man," concluded Mr. Thorn.

"He's a nutter all right, but there's no need to be like that," said Nina.

"In a way, no. I agree with you. But on the other hand—"

"Look, Mr. Thorn, I've seen nut-cases. Lots of them. I'm one myself, aren't I?" Nina spoke with an air of great reasonableness. "But there's loonies and loonies. They're all just people, aren't they? Some of them are bastards to start with, and if they go barmy it only makes them more so. And others are all right and you can tell they are, even if they're washing their hands every five minutes or walking backwards because they're afraid of their shadow following them. It doesn't matter how daft people get. It shows through, what a person really is. That one up there—" she jerked her head over her shoulder—"is one of the first sort. He's never had any sort of decent feelings at all. He'd be a rotten sort of character even if there was nothing the matter with him."

She spoke with a quaint sort of primness that Mr. Thorn found touching and even a little amusing, though, in fact, there was nothing in the situation to be amused about. He made a further effort to explain and defend Gerry's attitude, but it was not very convincing, even to himself. He had been very much struck by the girl's division of people into irreversible categories and by her forthright rejection of mental illness as an excuse for disagreeable behaviour.

"Nina," he said, when it was obvious that nothing was going to make her feel more kindly disposed towards Gerry, "do you really believe people ought to be judged as good or bad whatever their circumstances? However ill they are? However unlucky they have been in life?"

"Yes," she said without hesitation.

"Then if somebody goes and bashes an old lady in the park and pleads that it's because he had a miserable childhood, you'd say it was no excuse for his behaviour?"

"Of course it's no excuse!" she cried vehemently. "Lots of people have miserable childhoods, but they don't go knocking other people about because of it."

"Yes, yes. You're quite right, of course." Mr. Thorn was somewhat taken aback. "But we have to try to understand it all the same. We have to try to be charitable. After all, even the law, a very blunt instrument at best, makes a distinction between those who are responsible for their actions and those who aren't."

Mr. Thorn was talking as much to himself as to Nina. He had found her remarks rather disturbing, particularly as coming from one who had herself had an atrociously unhappy childhood but who, so Dorothy assured him, had never committed any acts of violence against other people or other people's possessions. The Reverend William Thorn, MA, with a lifetime of ministering to the needs of the poor, the sick, the bewildered, and the outright bloody-minded behind him, found himself feeling curiously humble in the presence of this sixteen-year-old waif who had formed such strong moral judgements without the benefit of a good home, or a good example, or a decent education to support her.

"That one knows what he's doing all right," said Nina, and again her eyes went upwards to indicat Gerry, presumably still quietly resting on the floor above.

"But what did he actually say to you to upset you so much?" asked Mr. Thorn.

"It wasn't what was said. It was the way he said it." And Nina, perhaps involuntarily, perhaps with deliberate malice, raised her eyebrows, looked down her nose, and tilted her head very slightly to one side as she spoke, in such unmistakable mimicry of Gerry's most supercilious manner that it gave Mr. Thorn another little shock and almost made him smile. He was very hard put to it to find an answer. He had disliked his son-in-law from the very first, but had kept these feelings to himself in the face of Dorothy's evident infatuation with Gerry. Even when Gerry was at his best, Mr. Thorn's charitable feelings towards him had been achieved only at the cost of much prayer and self-discipline. But since the revelation of what Dorothy had been going through, Mr. Thorn had been rather neglecting these strenuous efforts to be fair to Gerry and had been letting his detestation of the man have its full fling.

He was in no position to preach to Nina, he reflected guiltily. And yet something had got to be done. And quickly, because Gerry would be waking up soon and Dorothy would be coming home. What Gerry would say and do to her could be guessed at but not prevented. Nina, however, was more malleable. Nina must be worked on at once.

"I know how you feel and I can imagine how it was," said Mr. Thorn. "I've often felt like that myself as a matter of fact. But there's my daughter to be considered first and foremost. We have to keep quiet for her sake. It's an awful effort, but it's got to be done. You wouldn't want her to be made unhappy about it, would you, Nina?"

This appeal received a grudging assent. "He wants me to take him up some tea at half past four," added Nina.

"It's nearly that now. Hadn't you better go and make it?"

Suddenly Nina began to cry. "I was going to make a goulash for dinner," she wailed. "It's too late to start now. It needs ages to simmer. And besides . . ."

There was no need for her to explain any further. It was only too obvious that the homecoming of the master of the house was not an occasion to be celebrated with special culinary efforts.

"Perhaps we could have it another day," said Mr. Thorn.

"Not for him! I'm not going to cook anything for him!"

"But you want to help my daughter, don't you?"

Nina's expression would have been laughable if there had been anything to laugh at in the situation. Adoration of Dorothy and hatred of Gerry fought with each other to produce an appearance of total confusion.

"Of course you do," said Mr. Thorn. "So do I. That's why I am here. I have a flat of my own, you know, and I'd rather be living there. But it's better for my daughter to have other people in the house. Of course, if you really can't stand it, we will have to find somewhere else for you to live and someone else to do the work here, but—"

He broke off. At the mention of leaving Dorothy, horror had taken precedence over all other emotions in Nina's face.

"In that case you will just have to come to terms with it," said Dorothy's father firmly. "Just as I've had to do. We're in the same boat, Nina, you and I. We've got the same problem. And that means we can help each other. Now you go and make that tea and take some upstairs and then bring the tray in here. Will you do that, please? For Dorothy and for me?"

"All right." Nina got up despondently and left the room.

Mr. Thorn lay back and shut his eyes. His body was relaxed and he was breathing slowly and regularly. But the turmoil in his mind could not be stilled.

The new and unknown factor, he was saying to himself. And what a factor! Explosive, no less. Was it his fault? Was it Dorothy's? Ah well, he concluded, there was no turning back now.

—●14●—

The tension between Gerry and Nina electrified the whole house.

"It positively sizzles," said Dorothy to Peter. "It's a pity you can't come and de-fuse it."

She was sitting in his most comfortable armchair and although she looked tired after the long afternoon session at hospital there was an air of almost desperate cheerfulness about her. It was the third time in the ten days since Gerry had come home that she had called in on Peter after work. He had only just got in himself and they relaxed in a companionable way.

"What part of your timetable is this coming out of?" she asked him teasingly. "Or have you decided to allow yourself half an hour a day for sundries?"

"If we have some coffee it can count as shopping and eating, etc.," said Peter in the same tone of voice. "No. You sit there. I'm the host."

He produced coffee and biscuits. Dorothy declined the latter.

"I daren't eat anything before dinner," she said. "I have to save up every bit of my capacity to do justice to Nina.

She counts every mouthful I take, like an overanxious mother watching the progress of an underweight baby. I have to be careful not to gobble for fear she comes and pats my back to bring up the wind."

"It's not doing you any harm, though," said Peter, "being fed properly. You don't look quite so hag-ridden as when I first saw you."

"I don't know whether that's due to Nina's cooking or to the fact that for much of the time now I feel totally irresponsible. Everything seems to be completely out of control as far as my domestic life is concerned. I haven't the slightest doubt that something frightful is going to happen, but I no longer feel as if I can do anything to prevent it. The boat's lost its rudder. Or rather the rudder has been taken over by two equally determined pairs of hands, pulling with equal force in totally opposite directions. I'm just the donkey doing the rowing."

"As long as they don't tear you to pieces between them," said Peter.

"There's a certain amount of that, of course, and sometimes it is a bit harrowing. Meal times are the worst. But it's no worse than when I had Gerry to cope with on my own. You see, I'm not there for a lot of the time. My poor father bears the brunt of it."

"How is he standing up to it?"

"Pretty well on the whole. He had a little attack yesterday evening and Nina fussed over him like a mother hen."

Dorothy had certainly spoken the truth when she said she was feeling irresponsible, thought Peter; she would never have referred so lightly to Mr. Thorn's state of health two weeks ago. He was pleased but at the same time rather anxious: the change of mood was too sudden and too violent; it could so easily swing back again.

"Well, that's one comfort," he said stolidly. "That Nina and your father have made friends, I mean."

"Oh, they're thick as thieves. They have long conversations about moral philosophy. Dad's quite taken with her. He can't decide whether she's going to turn into an actress or into some sort of missionary."

"It sounds to me as if she ought to make a career out of catering."

"I expect it will come to that in the end." Dorothy got up. "Well, I must go. Thanks for letting me come and natter, Peter."

"You're welcome. Any time. Always."

After she had gone Peter told himself that yet again she had managed to avoid saying anything specific about Gerry. Was this because Gerry was concentrating his forces on the battle with Nina and had little energy left to direct at his wife? It would be nice to believe this, but Peter was sceptical. There was no doubt, however, that for the time being at least, Dorothy's life might have been worse.

Fortified by this comforting reflection, Peter pushed aside the coffee cups, slit open the bulky envelope of study material that had arrived that morning, and tried to devote himself to the mysteries of the Open University foundation course in Mathematics, which he was taking concurrently with that in Technology. It was tough going and required every bit of his power of concentration, undisturbed by any speculation about what was going on at Pond Cottage, Middle Lane, Hampstead.

Meal times are the worst, Dorothy had said. The hour before dinner, in particular, was crackling with anticipation. Nina's loathing of Gerry had, among less fortunate effects, that of spurring her on to ever more ambitious efforts in the kitchen—a sort of flaunting of her own skill and usefulness as opposed to Gerry's idle and pointless existence. Sometimes these efforts were successful and sometimes they were not. If Mr. Thorn said that a dish was overseasoned for his taste, or that on medical advice he would have to avoid it, Nina would accept his comment without taking offence and would make a mental note not to give it to him again. If something had gone so disastrously wrong that even

Dorothy, with all her concern for Nina's feelings, felt unable to eat the offering, then there were long and tearful apologies and a great deal of comforting had to be done by Dorothy and her father. Gerry, on these occasions, would take no part in the proceedings, but would sit with a satisfied smile on his face, watching and biding his time.

It was when Gerry, alone among those present, decided to make some adverse comment on Nina's cooking that the fireworks really began.

When Dorothy got home at about seven o'clock she found what looked like an idyllic scene for a summer evening. Gerry and her father were stretched out in garden chairs near the copper beech tree, a table with glasses and a jug between them, and a comfortable scatter of books and newspapers on the grass by their sides. Gerry had accepted Mr. Thorn's presence in the house with very little surprise and no protest: Nina was the arch enemy.

Dorothy left the car in the drive and came to sit in the vacant chair.

"It's been quite a day," she said. "Can we really be going to have a good summer after all?"

"The long-range forecast," said Mr. Thorn, after glancing at his paper, "is for below-average temperatures and above-average rainfall except in the north-west of Scotland."

"Bad luck on Scotland," said Dorothy lazily. "It's bound to be the other way round."

"You are looking very weary, my dear," said Gerry who had been silently observing Dorothy up till now. "Did you have a particularly exhausting session with your lover?"

Mr. Thorn's grip on his newspaper tightened involuntarily, but Dorothy appeared to be unmoved.

"Oh yes, frightfully exhausting," she replied lightly. "But then I took in six of them, you know, one after the other, after I'd finished the afternoon clinic."

Gerry's eyes narrowed. This was a new technique on Dorothy's part and so far he had not found the perfect

answer to it. But that Dorothy found it an effort to employ
this method of dealing with him was shown by the
thoughtlessness of her next remark.

"I wonder what Nina's making for dinner," she said.
"I'm ravenous."

"For how long," asked Gerry with an air of weary
resignation, "are our digestions to be at the mercy of that
adolescent delinquent? I fear it cannot be much longer
before she decides to work off her grudge against society in
general and against the bourgeoisie in particular by dropping a taste of arsenic in the soup. It did taste a little odd last
night, to say the least of it."

This speech was not up to Gerry's usual standard of
needling Dorothy or anybody else he wanted to take it out
on, and Dorothy herself had no difficulty in simply ignoring
it. But it got under Mr. Thorn's skin to such an extent that he
broke his rule of never rising to Gerry's baits.

"For somebody who has met with so little human
affection and suffered so much from human neglect," he
said with spite, "Nina is remarkably free of any grudge
against anybody."

Gerry looked at first faintly surprised and then delighted.
"Well, well," he said. "So the child has a champion."

Suddenly Dorothy could not bear to listen any longer.
She jumped to her feet, cried, "I want a wash," and ran into
the house. In the hall she met Nina, who was coming out of
the kitchen to say that things had got a little delayed and
would it be all right if they ate fifteen minutes later than
usual.

"Good," said Dorothy. "That'll give me time for a bath.
I'm feeling thoroughly hot and mucky."

"You don't look it," said Nina. "You look lovely."

The adoration in her voice was almost painful to hear.
Dorothy said lightly, "Thank you," and was about to go
upstairs when some impulse made her turn back. The girl
ran towards her and for a moment they clung together as

they had done on the occasion when Dorothy had suggested that Nina should come and live there.

I'm sure she knows, said Dorothy to herself as she ran the bath; there's some sort of telepathy that's told her I have lost a daughter, although of course I shall never tell her myself. And she's got an instinct about Gerry too. It's not only that she is competing with him for me. It's more than that. And Gerry knows too. How much longer will it be before one of us mentions Irene? Gerry must be thinking of her; he must. She would have been about Nina's age now. Did I take in Nina because I knew it would force Gerry and me to talk about Irene? I suppose that was it; I suppose that's why I feel better now, because I've taken some action at last, done something that is bound to force both Gerry and me into facing the truth together . . .

Dorothy's thoughts drifted on. It was quite true, as she had told Peter, that she was feeling oddly irresponsible. It was almost as if she was watching the whole domestic setup, herself included, from the stance of a detached observer, curious to know the end of the drama but not personally involved in it.

15

The meal was at first a very silent one. They ate in the dining area of the large kitchen and Dorothy thought she could detect a smell of fried onions, although none were present in the harmless but rather ordinary chicken dish and salad that Nina produced. Probably they had been in whatever it was that went wrong and had to be thrown away, thought Dorothy, and hoped Gerry would not come to the same conclusion and make a comment on it.

Gerry appeared to be eating somewhat absent-mindedly. His eyes were as often upon Dorothy, sitting opposite to him, as on his plate. When Nina got up to put a raspberry flan on the table, Gerry, still staring at Dorothy, said in a speculative manner, "Curious. I never thought you would resurrect that dress again. It's so very much not your style. It needs a bit of youthful glamour to carry it off. Or if not glamour, at any rate a modicum of beauty and charm."

The rather frilly summer dress did indeed look wrong on Dorothy, who needed simple, even austere clothes to achieve her odd flashes of something like beauty. She had only put it on because it was cool and comfortable and the first thing that had come to hand.

"Do I look like mutton dressed as lamb?" she said good-humouredly. "I seem to be short of summer clothes. I'll have to get some more if the weather goes on like this."

And she smiled at her father to show that this sort of thing did not worry her.

But it worried Nina, who was already upset by the failure of the sauce she had been attempting and who had indeed felt, when she and Dorothy had momentarily hugged each other, something of the older woman's deeply suppressed yearning and despair.

Gerry reached out for the sugar, which was at the corner of the table nearest Nina's seat. Without a word Nina suddenly bent over and bit his bare forearm.

It was not a very hard bite. As quickly as Nina's head had ducked it came up again and she stared, white-faced and cringing, at Dorothy. Gerry did not even trouble to move his arm or touch the spot. He picked up the sugar canister and sprinkled sugar over the raspberries before he began to eat. For a full minute there was silence. Then Gerry said conversationally, "I was not aware, Dolly, that it came within the scope of the Hippocratic Oath, nor that it was accepted medical practice even today, to treat violent mental patients by giving them privileged positions in the practitioner's own home."

"It isn't." Dorothy's voice held such fury and menace that her father looked at her in alarm and Nina looked more terrified than ever. "Except," continued Dorothy with deadly clarity, "when the violent mental patient happens to be the practitioner's own husband. In that case she has no choice."

Gerry got up, came round the table, and hit her with considerable force across the side of the head. Dorothy gave an involuntary cry of pain. Nina shrieked and sprang at Gerry. Dorothy's father, instantly judging this to be an occasion when his own carefully conserved energies would have to be brought into action, jumped up and caught hold of Nina before she could either touch Gerry or Gerry her.

Nina struggled hard but Mr. Thorn held her. To his great relief Gerry left the room. But Nina clearly wanted to run after him.

"No," gasped Mr. Thorn. "It will do—no good."

His breathing was becoming very laboured but he continued to hold Nina back. Dorothy, recovering from the shock of the blow and seeing his condition, cried, "Stop that at once, Nina! Can't you see my father is ill? Help me to get him to bed. At once!"

The voice of authority had its effect, helped by the old man's rapidly increasing distress. Nina ceased to struggle and asked what she could do to help. The next two hours were very busy and very anxious. Mr. Thorn's own doctor was summoned and agreed with Dorothy that it would be better not to risk moving the old man to hospital, although he would need constant care and attention. At that point Nina begged to be allowed to look after him. Dorothy surveyed her doubtfully.

"He must not be excited in any way," said Dr. Ferguson.

"I won't excite him. I'll keep him quiet. Truly I will!" cried Nina,

"All right," said Dorothy at last. "I shall be here too. I shall take a few days' leave. You can start by sitting with him now, Nina, while I show Dr. Ferguson out."

When Dorothy came upstairs again after a few final words with Mr. Thorn's doctor, she stood for a moment in the doorway of her father's room. The curtains were drawn across, but the short summer night had not yet begun and there was enough light to see that the old man was lying peacefully asleep, breathing lightly but evenly. The oxygen equipment stood at one side of the bed. At the other side Nina knelt with her eyes on the old man's face. Her elbows rested on the edge of the bed and her hands were clasped together as if she were praying. Dorothy silently withdrew, leaving the door slightly ajar. Then she went in search of Gerry.

He had not gone to bed, neither was he in the bathroom or

in any of the spare bedrooms. Dorothy went downstairs and tried the door of the study. It did not open.

"Gerry," she called softly. "It's all right. My father is better now. The doctor has gone."

There was no reply.

"Are you coming to bed?" she asked and then held her ear close to the door. There was not the slightest sound from within the room.

Dorothy rattled the doorhandle. "Don't be silly," she said in a harsh whisper, fearful that she might disturb her father on the floor above. "I know you're there and I know you're all right. You wouldn't take an overdose of anything without making sure I could get at you to bring you round. Open the door, Gerry. This has gone on long enough."

Dead silence followed this speech.

"All right then," said Dorothy. "Stay there. I shall go to bed."

And she let go of the handle and stood still for a moment or two without speaking, to give the impression that she had indeed gone away. When this produced no reaction she began for the first time to be seriously anxious. Curiously enough, the anxiety no longer took the form of a struggle between her own desire to find Gerry dead and her fear of her own guilt if she were to do so. She was conscious only of great weariness and an intense reluctance to deal with any more emergencies tonight. For this reason she found herself positively hoping that he was alive and uninjured so that, medically at least, there would be nothing she need do. If he had harmed himself, she hoped it would simply be a case of a few sleeping tablets too many, which could be quickly dealt with by giving salt water as an emetic.

But if he was really in danger, which would mean all the fuss of an ambulance, or if he was dead, which would mean sending for Dr. Ferguson again and perhaps for the police, Dorothy did not know how she would find the energy to cope with it.

Why not just go to bed?

She was almost able to do this, but not quite. The habit of years died very hard. She thought for a moment and then decided to try to get at Gerry through the window of the study, which he must surely have left open on so hot a night as this. She collected a small stepladder from the broom-cupboard and left the house by the back door, still taking care to make as little noise as possible, and grateful that her father's room was on the other side of the house.

There was no light coming from Gerry's study, but one of the casement windows was wide open and the curtains were drawn only half across. Dorothy stood on the third rung of the stepladder and leant on the sill.

"Gerry!" she called softly. "Are you going to open the door now or do I have to climb in?"

There was no reply. She could see him dimly, sitting in the desk chair with his arms on the desk and his head buried in his arms. Whether or not he was breathing was impossible to tell in the near darkness.

Dorothy took a further step up the ladder and put one knee on the windowsill. It was possible to get in, although it would require an awkward manoeuvre, because the desk was pushed against the wall directly in front of the window, and she could not simply fling a leg over the sill and then drop down on to the floor. She would have to shuffle or crawl on to the desk on her knees, and if Gerry was alive and conscious and was simply playing with her, which was perfectly possible, then for a moment or two at least she would be in a very vulnerable position.

But there was no help for it. Dorothy got both knees on to the sill and crawled forward on to the desk. She had turned round and was about to slide to the floor when a hand shot out and grabbed her ankle and a triumphant voice cried: "Got you!"

For all her preparedness, Dorothy could not suppress a little scream.

"What the hell are you playing at?" she cried. "Didn't you hear me at the door?"

"Yes. I heard you."

"Then why didn't you open it?"

Dorothy shook herself free and walked over to switch on the light. Gerry was lolling back in the desk chair, surveying her with an expression of great malevolence.

"Very interesting, that little experiment," he said. "It proves that it is perfectly possible for you to enter this room in an unorthodox manner. So that when my body is found it will not necessarily present the police with an insoluble locked room mystery. The murderer, having locked the door on the inside in order to suggest suicide, then made her way out of the room through the window. That is one point settled. The method? Ah, there's the rub. What method can be adopted that will point directly and exclusively to Dr. Dorothy Laver? This is quite a problem. But we will find an answer, given patience and time, patience and time, patience and time . . ."

He continued to repeat the words, beating a little rhythm with one hand as if conducting an orchestra.

"Perhaps we could defer until the morning our discussion of the means whereby I am to be convicted of your murder," said Dorothy. "I think you'd better come and rest now."

Her voice sounded calm and firm, the doctor dealing with a difficult and excitable patient. But, in fact, she was not at all confident of being able to manage him on her own as she had always done in the past. His whole pattern of behaviour had changed. He seemed less subtle and less cunning in his choice of disagreeable things to say, less in control of both his words and his actions.

Involuntarily Dorothy put a hand to her face: Gerry had never actually struck her before. He noticed her gesture, came and put an arm round her and stroked her hair.

"I'm sorry I hurt you, Dolly," he said. "That was naughty of me. But it was naughty of you too, wasn't it, to make such unkind remarks in front of other people. And now you've gone and made your father ill. All because you couldn't control your naughty tongue. Poor Bill. Suppose he should die? It will be your fault, won't it, Dolly? Naughty Dolly. Unlucky Dolly. She keeps losing people. And it's always her own fault. Her father . . . her daughter . . . and now her husband."

Dorothy stiffened. Gerry continued to stroke her hair.

"And her husband, which won't be much loss," he said. "Everyone will say—that wretched man, making her life such a misery, such a burden to her, how good that she's free of him at last. But you won't be free, will you, my darling Dolly, because they'll know you killed me and even if you manage to get acquitted because you've made them believe it was an accident, it will still be a life sentence because you'll never forget, never forget, never forget . . ."

Again he went on repeating the words, this time to the rhythm of the movement of his hand over her hair. Dorothy pulled herself away with a jerk, backed towards the door, leant against it and felt for the handle and cried: "We both killed Irene. Both of us, both of us, both of us . . ."

It seemed as if she, too, had to keep saying the same words over and over again. At last she managed to stop herself and stood clinging to the doorhandle and trembling uncontrollably. It's come at last, she thought; this is the end now. There is no more pretence. One of us has to admit to having killed our child. And one of us has to die.

As usual, having driven her to the verge of collapse, Gerry began to recover his own composure. In this respect it was just the same as it had always been. It was as if between them there was only enough calmness and sanity for one person. Whichever one of them possessed it was automatically depriving the other.

"That was certainly the intention that the coroner intended to convey," said Gerry, and his voice had never sounded more schoolmasterly and precise. "A tragic accident arising from a misunderstanding. Deep sympathy for the bereaved parents. Impossible to apportion blame, or indeed to blame anybody at all. Accidents will happen. It is the way of life."

Dorothy tried to speak. Her mouth opened and shut but no words came. Her one short outburst had exhausted all her powers.

"A tragic accident arising from a misunderstanding, and deep sympathy for the bereaved parents," repeated Gerry slowly and emphatically, as if he was trying to get a difficult point across to a not very intelligent pupil. "That was the impression left by the inquest, and that was the story for public consumption thereafter. But you and I know that it was not true, don't we, Dolly? We know that you have always felt solely responsible for Irene's death, don't we? We know that you believe you killed Irene. Am I not right, Dorothy?"

"Yes, that's right," muttered Dorothy. And then she added more firmly, "I've always felt responsible because I believed you when you told me it was I who had made the mistake. It has only been in recent years . . ."

Her voice faded away.

"What have you been thinking in recent years?" asked Gerry in the same tones of weary patience.

Dorothy did not look at him because she did not want to see the expression in his eyes. She was becoming very frightened indeed but there was no drawing back now. She had gone too far.

"I have been wondering whether it wasn't you who was to blame," she went on hurriedly. "Whether it wasn't because you had killed Irene that you felt you had to kill yourself . . . whether you'd been torturing me all these years to try to stop me suspecting the truth."

"Can I be hearing aright?" said Gerry in his most sarcastic manner. "Me torturing you? What a very peculiar way to look at it. Which one of us has had an unbroken and successful career and has reached a position of considerable eminence in it? And which one of us has suffered a serious mental breakdown with severe residual symptoms in the form of suicidal impulses? I had rather been under the impression that the former description applied to my wife and the latter to myself. But in addition to losing my daughter through my wife's carelessness, in addition to allowing myself to be partially blamed, and in addition to suffering serious illness and the ruin of my career, it appears that I am also to be deprived of the one consolation left to me—that of knowing myself to be the more unfortunate of the two of us."

Dorothy clamped her hands over her ears as if to shut out an intolerable noise.

"Stop it, stop it!" she cried. "My mind is reeling. Which of us is crazy—you or me?"

Gerry shrugged his shoulders, pulled the chair out from the desk, sat down, and took up a book that apparently he had been reading earlier.

Suddenly something snapped in Dorothy. She no longer possessed a controlling mind: She was all blind impulse. She rushed at Gerry, caught hold of his shoulders, and shook him hard.

"You killed her!" she screamed. "It was you—you—you!"

Gerry caught her hands and held them down. "My dear Dorothy," he said, "I really think you had better make an effort to control yourself. You might be overheard, which would be very embarrassing for you."

"I don't care who hears!" cried Dorothy.

"Don't you? Do you really want your father and your daughter-substitute to suffer for your sins as well as yourself?"

Suddenly Dorothy stood quite still. "You wouldn't—you couldn't—you wouldn't harm them," she whispered.

"I have protected you all these years from the consequences of your criminal negligence," said Gerry, "at great cost to myself. I think it is time now to redress the balance and give myself a chance."

Dorothy shut her eyes for a moment. Then she opened

them again and said very quietly, "Why don't you just kill me, Gerry, if that's what would make you happy? Go on. Strangle me."

A cunning look came into his face. "Ah no. That's what *you* want, isn't it? They'd get me if I did that, wouldn't they? You're determined to make me into a murderer one way or the other, aren't you, Doll, even if you have to die for it. No, no. That's not what I want."

"Then what is?"

"I think we will have a reversal of roles for a change. We've had enough of the heroic Dr. Laver and her mad husband. I think we will have the mad Dr. Laver and her so very calm and coping husband."

Again Dorothy shut her eyes. "All right. If that's the way you want it," she said softly.

—16—

Three days later Peter had a telephone call from Bill Thorn.

"Thank God you're there," said the old man's voice when Peter lifted the receiver.

It was six-thirty in the evening, and Len Hardy had gone home. Peter had come into their combined office and workshop for a few minutes to collect some materials for a rewiring job that he was starting early the following morning.

"Are you all right?" he asked. The old man sounded very breathless.

"Yes. I've been ill, but I'm much better now. Just give me a moment."

Peter waited anxiously.

"I really am all right," said Bill Thorn a moment later. "That was a tactical silence—somebody passing by. Are you free this evening and if so, can you come round to see Dorothy?"

"Of course. D'you mean come to Pond Cottage?"

"Yes. She's not feeling very well. Don't worry. Gerry won't be here. Seven-thirty. Not earlier."

"I'll be there," promised Peter, and again there was a

silence, which was broken eventually by Mr. Thorn saying in a rather plaintive voice, "I'm so sorry, my dear fellow, but I'm afraid I can't take on any locum jobs nowadays. Health isn't up to it. My preaching days are over. Glad you tracked me down, though. I'll be staying with my daughter a little longer and will get in touch with you when I go home. Perhaps we can meet for a chat some time. Goodbye."

The line went dead. Peter, after the first bewildered moment, wondered whether he ought to have disguised his voice and pretended to be some clerical acquaintance of Bill Thorn's. It was obvious that the last sentences had been intended for the benefit of whoever was now overhearing the conversation.

But would Gerry be so easily taken in, wondered Peter. For surely it could only be Gerry who must not know that a call was being made to Peter. On the other hand, Bill had said that Gerry was not there. Where then could he be? And Dorothy was not feeling well. Was that Bill's tactful way of saying she was very ill? Had Gerry injured her in some way, and been committed to hospital himself?

With his mind swarming with questions, Peter finished his business, locked up the shop, and drove slowly in the direction of Hampstead, taking care not to arrive at Pond Cottage even half a minute too early. It seemed a long time before anybody came to answer the bell. The road was very quiet, almost uncannily so. There was a faint distant hum of traffic, and several streets away somebody was practising the flute, but otherwise blackbirds and thrushes held full sway. It was difficult to imagine a greater contrast to Victoria Avenue than this exclusive little leafy enclave, with its pink chestnut trees and white-painted balconies and shiny metal burglar alarms.

Peter had his own dream of an ideal home and every intention of trying to realize it. Nevertheless he could not help wondering for a moment whether the semi-slum in which he was now living was not in some respects a healthier neighbourhood than the one where Dorothy lived and suffered. How much more domestic misery lay locked away in these discreetly luxurious homes?

His mind had slithered on to a ridiculously idealistic picture of himself and Dorothy in some superbly designed modern bungalow on the outskirts of a south coast town, when at last the door was opened.

"Ah. There you are. Come in here, please," said Bill Thorn.

In the blue-and-white sitting-room Peter asked at once, "Where's Dorothy?"

"In the consulting-room. She's using it as a bedroom and is resting there. You'll find her changed. Let me explain before you see her. We've plenty of time. Gerry is out all evening."

Mr. Thorn lowered himself slowly into a chair before continuing. "I'm sorry," he said. "I can't hurry. I've been rather ill."

He did indeed look more gaunt and frail than ever. Peter expressed concern. Bill Thorn waved it aside. "I'll be all right," he said. "These turns are alarming, but I soon recover. Until the final one comes, of course, but I don't think that will be just yet."

And he proceeded to relate in detail the events leading up to his recent attack.

"At that point I was no longer able to take an active part in the proceedings," he concluded. "The following day I was also not very much aware of what was going on, although I know Dr. Ferguson came a couple of times and I believe Nina scarcely left my room. No one could have had a better nurse. I saw nothing of Gerry and next to nothing of Dorothy. I believe I did think it odd that she only looked in to ask whether Nina was looking after me and didn't seem to want to attend to my needs herself."

"That's not like Dorothy at all," agreed Peter.

"No, but I thought perhaps she was doing it for Nina's sake—letting the girl see how well she could cope. It was another night and half a day before I had recovered enough to realize that something was very wrong."

Mr. Thorn paused for a moment to rest himself and Peter waited silently in wretched anxiety.

"Something must have happened between Gerry and Dorothy that night," went on Bill at last, "and I want you to find out what it was. She says nothing. In fact, she does nothing—just lies on the couch all day. It was actually Gerry who rang the hospital to say she was ill and who asked them to make arrangements for someone else to see her private patients as well. It's years since he has been capable of such decisive action. He has also made it plain to me, quite politely, that I shall not be welcome here for much longer, and as soon as I am completely recovered I am expected to go. While as for Nina—"

Again Mr. Thorn had to take a little rest before continuing.

"I don't know what Gerry's intentions are with regard to Nina. I imagine to get rid of her, but it may be that he is waiting until I am out of the way. Or he may be intending to make use of her in some way connected with Dorothy. At the moment he is completely ignoring her and she him. It's very odd, but at least it's peaceful."

"But what can have come over him?" cried Peter. "Is he suddenly cured? Is it possible for that sort of condition suddenly to work itself out in this way?"

"I've no idea," said Bill. "Dorothy would know, but she's not in a fit state to ask. He certainly seems to be going through some sort of active phase, but whether it's permanent or not . . . I'm inclined to think not. I suppose Dorothy would call it the manic phase of a manic-depressive cycle. That's the jargon, isn't it? I expect he's had such fits before, but I don't think they can have resulted in quite such a burst of activity. And they certainly have never had an effect like this on Dorothy. Nothing ever has. I have never seen her like this in my life. Even after her own grievous loss she never became as completely demoralized as this. She seems to have lost all will to live. I'm relying on you, Peter, to bring it back to her."

"I can only do my best," muttered Peter, getting to his feet.

Mr. Thorn rose too. "Yes, we will go to see her now. Nina is upstairs at the moment, but she'll bring some coffee later on."

"And Gerry?"

"Gerry has gone out to dinner with Dorothy's old schoolfriend Pauline, who was at one time a friend of his. She is now a wealthy widow. An over-sweet lady. I don't trust her. Gerry phoned her the day after I became ill. That is also something he has never done before, to my knowledge. She bustled round full of sympathy for everyone and terribly anxious to help. Very inquisitive. Very determined that Dorothy's nervous collapse should be made much of. Very keen to advise Gerry about what to do with her. I imagine this little dinner-party is to discuss the situation at Pond Cottage. Lots of sympathy for poor Gerry. God knows what they are cooking up between them. Or what he is telling her about Dorothy."

Peter gave a short angry laugh. "Telling Pauline he's got a mad wife, no doubt," he said. "I suppose he's trying to dump his neurosis on Dorothy."

They moved to the door.

"It seems so, it seems so," said Bill.

Peter glanced at him and for the first time that evening caught the full measure of the old man's distress.

"You think Gerry is seriously trying to make out that it is Dorothy who is out of her mind?" he asked.

Bill Thorn nodded. "But it doesn't matter if he manages to convince Pauline. Or anyone else for that matter. That can be dealt with in due course. The essential thing is that he doesn't succeed in convincing Dorothy herself. That's where you come in. To find out exactly what has happened between them and to get it across to her that she is perfectly

sane. She's not simply exhausted, Peter. She's very frightened indeed. That's not like her, and I want to know why."

After the sunny blue-and-white room, Dorothy's consulting-room, with the long wall of books and the desk and the
filing cabinet, looked austere and even sombre. It also
looked to Peter rather larger than it had done on the evening
when he had helped to carry Gerry in there. But that might
have been because Dorothy herself seemed so small and
shrunken. Cushions and pillows had been piled at one end
of the couch and she was curled up against them. She was
barelegged and was wearing a rather crumpled cotton dress.
Her black hair was untidy and straggly, as if it had been
dampened and was hanging in rat's tails, and her eyes were
dull. A plain woman. Sick, weary, and defeated. Every
little spark of that vitality that had so attracted Peter seemed
to have been extinguished. Had he met her now for the first
time he could have felt no stronger emotion than pity.

He felt pity now, but also fury at whoever or whatever
had done this to her. If there was anything on earth he could
do to restore Dorothy to her former self, he would do it, at
whatever cost to himself or to anybody else.

Dorothy put down the evening paper and looked up at
him.

"Hullo, Peter," she said. "I thought I heard your voice.
Did my father ask you to come?"

She sounded very listless but quite normal. Peter felt
immense relief. For a horrible moment he had feared that
her mind had been so affected that she would not recognize
him.

"He told me you weren't very well," said Peter, coming
to sit on the end of the couch. "I hope you don't mind me
coming to see you."

"Not a bit. It's very kind of you," said Dorothy formally.
"I'm sorry I can't entertain you in any way, but I'm almost
too feeble to walk across the room. I seem to be having
some sort of nervous collapse. Not what you'd expect of a
psychiatrist. Funny, isn't it?"

"I suppose doctors can fall ill just like anybody else," said Peter. "Have you consulted anybody about it? Or are you prescribing for yourself?"

Dorothy did not reply to this direct. "There's nothing much to be done," she said vaguely. "Just rest. Try not to worry. Try not to get over-excited."

Peter asked several more questions about herself but she answered them all in the same uninformative manner. It seemed to him that she was deliberately spinning a web about herself, keeping him at bay. If that was the case, then there must be some core of energy left in her, something of her own true self. But how was he to get through to it? The precious minutes were passing and he was getting nowhere.

"And what about you, Peter?" she asked presently. "How is all the studying going?"

He began to tell her about the course in Electromagnetics and Electronics that he had chosen to do the following year and that he was looking forward to because there would be less of the theory and more of the practical work, with which he was always happier. Previously she would have been interested, but he could see now that she was not really listening. Her eyes were open but they were turned inwards.

"I think you're marvellous to work so hard," she said. "I'm sure you're going to get to the top one day."

There was nothing of Dorothy's fervour and intelligence in the remark. It was as if she was playing the little woman, the ignorant female boosting the male ego, and it disgusted Peter so much that quite automatically, and without any planning, he did the best possible thing.

"Will you please stop that bloody silly act at once!" he said brutally. "It's not surprising that you're worn out after all the strain you've been through, but because your body and mind and emotions need a rest doesn't mean that you have to take leave of your wits!"

Dorothy put her hands over her face and shrank back against the pillows.

"I don't see why having a nervous collapse should make

people feeble-minded," continued Peter in the same tone of voice. "It didn't do it to Gerry. You said yourself that his intellect always continues to function, however crazy he is."

"Gerry isn't crazy," muttered Dorothy between her fingers. "It's been all my fault."

"Balls!" shouted Peter. "Will you stop talking such rubbish?" He caught hold of her hands and held them away from her face. "Now what's all this about? What's this hold over you that Gerry's got?"

Dorothy blinked and gave a little moan.

"I'm not going out of this house till you tell me," said Peter. "If Gerry comes back and tries to turn me out, then we'll have another fight, that's all. If he gets hold of a knife, then I'll grab one too."

"A knife?" murmured Dorothy questioningly. The dull look had gone out of her eyes and she looked both startled and puzzled.

"Yes. A knife. Don't try to pretend you've forgotten. That crazy husband of yours went for me with a very sharp breadknife. If you look above my right eye you'll see the scar. You cleaned it and disinfected it yourself. Fortunately no stitches were required."

Dorothy was shuddering and grimacing all the time that Peter was speaking. It was painful to watch, as if somebody was coming round out of an anaesthetic too soon. It was going to get worse, he had no doubt, but he could not turn back now: this sort of shock treatment was the only way.

"Yes," she said at last. "I remember."

"And while we were sitting on Hampstead Heath you told me about all the times he had tried to kill himself. Remember?"

"Yes."

"And then he got rid of Mrs. Oliver. And he left you a letter saying he was going to commit suicide and make it look as if you had murdered him. You showed me the letter.

And you showed it to your father. We both read it. It was not the letter of a sane man. Was it? Was it, Dorothy?"

He shook her a little and again she whispered an answer. "No."

"What happened the other night after your father had that attack?" went on Peter.

Dorothy made no reply.

"Did he threaten you that way again? Is that what you're afraid of?"

Peter waited but she still said nothing. "You know what the best answer to that threat is, don't you, Dorothy? It's just to clear right out of here, isn't it? If you're nowhere near him, then there's no way you could be suspected of killing him. But he's not going to kill himself. You know he isn't. He's gone and taken up with Pauline. She wanted him in the first place. You told me so. Let her have him. Let her take him on and the house too and you come away with me, Dorothy. Now. At once. Tonight."

"No, no." She was crying now. "I'm so tired."

"Yes, of course." Peter laid her back against the cushions, held her hand gently, and then hastened to retrieve his error of tactics. He had let his anxiety to get her out of this house at all costs run away with him and divert him from the attempt to find out what had happened. He believed that he had been making some progress and hoped that it was not too late to regain the position.

"You'll rest soon," he said, "and you'll rest much better when you've told me how Gerry is threatening you. I'm not going away from here until you tell me. I mean that, Dorothy. He hit you, didn't he? Your father told me. Is that what's worrying you? Or has he threatened Nina? Or your father? Or me?"

Peter persisted with each question until he got some sort of response, even if it was only a slight movement of the head that could not be interpreted as either a shake or a nod, but that did at least show that she had heard his question.

"Nina," he said thoughtfully. "Your taking in that girl

brought matters to a crisis. As if Gerry were a spoilt child who could not bear to share you with another . . . a spoilt child . . . a child . . . Dorothy," he said, leaning towards her and speaking very urgently, "was there ever a child?"

The spasm that controted her face gave him the answer. Bill Thorn's remark about her "grievous loss" came back to him and he knew he was getting to the heart of the matter at last.

"When?" he asked. "What happened?"

"Fifteen years ago. She died." Dorothy was weeping now but her words were quite audible.

"I'm sorry," said Peter very gently. "How did it happen?"

"I killed her," said Dorothy in the same clear low voice. "I gave her an overdose of a drug."

——17——

Peter managed to control his shock and say in steady, matter-of-fact tones, "Now we're getting somewhere. How did you come to make such a mistake? And was Gerry there at the time?"

The story came out jerkily and disjointedly but it was not too difficult to piece it together into a coherent whole.

"Was it proved beyond all doubt that the drug was responsible for her death?" Peter asked.

"No doubt at all. A colleague of mine carried out the post-mortem." Dorothy was now quite calm and still and hopeless; a witness for the defence knowing there was no way of avoiding a guilty verdict.

"But you didn't actually hold the cup for the child to drink from it?"

"No. Gerry did that. I'd been called to the telephone."

"Then couldn't it have been Gerry who made the mistake about the dose?"

"No. I'd already prepared it. I'd measured out the drops from the bottle into the orange juice. The phone call came as I was doing it. I was rather expecting a call from a patient who was very disturbed and in danger of harming himself.

Gerry answered the phone in the other room—we lived in a flat then. He came into the kitchen and said, 'Sounds like one of your dottier cases, Dolly.' I hadn't qualified in psychological medicine then. I was still training. I got very anxious if a patient looked like coming to serious harm. I wasn't particularly bothered about Irene at that moment. She'd had this nasty chest trouble, but it was clearing up well. The medicine she was taking was effective and perfectly safe . . . in the correct doses. The orange juice was to make it more palatable, although in her case . . ."

Dorothy's voice faltered for the first time.

"She was a good little patient," she said at last. "Took everything given her without making a fuss, even if it didn't taste very nice."

"So it was Gerry who actually gave the dose?" prompted Peter.

"Yes. He was quite good with her. We had a girl living in, but it was her evening off."

"It must have been a very tough time for you," said Peter, "doing a hard professional grind and with a young child to look after. Not to mention a husband who presumably made a lot of demands, even at that time."

"It was my own choice," said Dorothy. "It's overworked professional women who kill their babies."

"Nonsense." Peter gave her a little shake. "Snap out of that! If you were indeed responsible for measuring out too much of the drug, then it was nothing more than a most ghastly mistake, the sort of thing one does when thinking about too many things at once. But I'm not at all convinced that you were responsible. There are so many other possibilities. Couldn't Gerry have added the extra drops after you'd gone to answer the phone?"

"That's the story he told for the coroner. He said that he had understood me to say, as I went to the phone, that I hadn't put the drops in. When I gave my evidence I said that I had told Gerry I'd done the drops. They believed us, both of us. The verdict was accidental death. Everybody was very sympathetic."

"Your father?"

"That's the version of the story that he knows. And my mother too. She was alive then. And everybody else. Everyone has always believed that is what happened. You are the first person who has ever heard the truth. Apart from Gerry."

"I don't think I am hearing the truth now," said Peter firmly. "I believe the account that was given at the inquest was in fact the true one. I believe it is Gerry himself who has put this idea of your own guilt into you over the years. I've never learnt anything about psychology, but that seems to make sense. He felt guilty himself. He couldn't stand it. And he was jealous of you. You were more successful in your career than he was in his. You were more brilliant in every way. He worked hard at making you believe you were solely responsible for the child's death. But the strain on him has been very great. He's forced a lie on you for all these years, and now he is afraid you are going to reject that lie. So he has to force you into a collapse. If you give up fighting, then it lets him off. It proves his lie is true. There!" Peter finished triumphantly. "How's that for a piece of subtle psychological analysis on the part of a plodding student of technology?"

"Pretty good." Dorothy gave a wan smile. "I should give it an alpha minus."

It was a fleeting glimpse of the old Dorothy, and it gave Peter hope, although the hope faded again when she almost at once reverted to her obstinate, almost sullen manner.

"It's a pretty story but it isn't true," she said. "The truth is that I put the extra drops in myself."

"How can you be so sure? It's a long time ago and it's terribly easy to be mistaken about pills and things."

"Terribly easy. I was mistaken. My mind was on my patients, not on the child."

Peter tried another tack. "All right then. Let's suppose it

was really you who made the mistake. You felt guilty, at any rate, you felt as if you had done it. But haven't you paid for it over and over again? Haven't you served your sentence? Fifteen years is a long time. Longer than anybody would get for manslaughter. Don't you think it's time you came out of prison now?"

Dorothy shook her head. "I can't live with it any longer," she muttered.

A new and horrible suspicion came into Peter's mind. Could it possibly be that Gerry was trying to drive it to the bitter end? To push Dorothy to suicide? He fought down the suspicion. Dorothy would never give in; she would never take that way out.

"Of course you can't live with it any longer," he said robustly. "Isn't that exactly what I am saying? You've been punished enough. It's time to call a halt. And the only way to do that is to get you away from Gerry."

Again Dorothy shook her head.

"Good God, woman, haven't you any pride?" cried Peter. "How much longer do you want to act as whipping-girl?"

Dorothy began to cry again and Peter made a great effort to take a grip on himself. He stood up. "I think I'd better go and tell your father," he said. "He knows better than I do how to manage you."

"Don't tell my father!" Dorothy actually got up from the couch and clung to the table. She looked and sounded horrified.

"You ought to have told him about it ages ago," said Peter. "It would never have got to this point if you had."

"I couldn't . . . it would have hurt him so much . . . he's been so proud of me . . . and my career."

"When I see what a fool an intelligent person can be," exclaimed Peter, "it's almost enough to make me give up my academic ambitions."

"You mustn't do that!" cried Dorothy.

"No, I mustn't, must I, or you'll be feeling guilty about

that too. All right then. For the time being I won't tell your
father that Gerry has been morally blackmailing you for
years in this absolutely unspeakable manner. But I'll only
keep quiet on one condition."

Dorothy glanced at him apprehensively. She looked so
pitiful that Peter ached to comfort her but he kept saying to
himself: no, not yet. This is the only way.

"If I promise not to tell your father," he said, "will you
promise in return that you will make every effort to keep
yourself alive and to get well again?"

"I'm not well," she muttered.

"No, you are not well, but there's no need to make
yourself worse or to take any risks. You understand me,
don't you? Yes, I see you do. I'm warning you, Dr. Dorothy
Laver, if you go overdosing yourself or doing anything
idiotic like that, you'll be going to heaven or hell with the
whole of my own life's misery on your conscience. You
mean everything to me. I don't want to have to face my life
without you. And what about your father? What about all
your patients who depend so much on you? What about
your friends? What about Nina? What help will it be for
Irene who has long been dead if you take yourself away
from Nina who is alive and desperately needs you?"

Peter had never been so worked up in his life. He was
speaking with a passion and fervour that would have
astonished anybody who had ever known him. Dorothy said
nothing, but he had the feeling that his appeal had struck
home and would not be forgotten. Perhaps that was all he
could expect at the moment; perhaps he had better leave it at
that.

There was a knock at the door and he went to open it. The
girl who came in carrying a tray looked almost as white and
frightened as Dorothy did herself.

"You must be Nina," said Peter. "I'm Peter Tarrant and
I've been telling Dorothy she's got to look after herself."

Nina nodded vigorous approval as she poured out the
coffee.

"Here's my address, Nina," said Peter. "Two addresses—my work and my home. And here's my work phone number. If I'm not there Mr. Hardy will be and he'll know where I am. Here's my landlord's phone. He'll take a message or call me if it's a real emergency. I want you to get in touch with me immediately if anything happens here that you think I ought to know. Get me?"

"Yes," said Nina.

"Even if Dorothy says you need not."

"Yes," said Nina again.

They both looked at Dorothy. She had sat down again and was slowly shaking her head.

"And keep close watch on her," said Peter. "Whatever happens. Whoever tries to stop you."

"I am keeping watch!" cried Nina. "I come and sleep down here when *he's* gone to bed. In the other room. With the door open so I can hear."

"Good girl. Thanks for the coffee." Peter swallowed it in a couple of gulps. "Goodbye, Dorothy. Good luck. See you again soon."

He could not bear to look at her; he felt he had caused too much pain.

Bill Thorn was waiting anxiously in the blue-and-white room.

"She's told me about it," said Peter. "I've been bullying her horribly. I feel sick with myself."

"It will pass," said the old man. "Well?"

"I promised not to tell you," said Peter slowly. "Actually it doesn't really matter very much what it is. She feels guilty about something in the past—whether rightly or wrongly I don't know—and Gerry's been playing on it all these years. Just recently he's been stepping up the blackmail, putting on the pressure to an intolerable degree. That's why she's cracked up."

"The child," said Bill Thorn promptly. "It's obviously to do with the child's death."

"You know about it?"

"She's never talked to me about it," said Dorothy's father, "but it's not been difficult to guess that she feels herself completely to blame. I suppose Gerry has been encouraging that belief in order to have a hold over her. Is that it, Peter?"

"I promised I wouldn't tell you," said Peter.

"You haven't told me. I've guessed it. If it weren't that he is so obviously insane, that man would be an offence to humanity."

"What's worrying me . . ." began Peter and then stopped.

"Yes?" Bill Thorn looked very alert.

"I hope I haven't made things worse for her," said Peter. "With Gerry, I mean. By forcing her to tell me about the child."

"Go on," said Mr. Thorn grimly.

"If he finds out that she's told me, it could drive him into drastic action."

"Go on," said Bill Thorn again.

Peter jumped up and began to walk excitedly about the room. "Suppose—just suppose—that it was Gerry himself who killed the child. Perhaps by accident, perhaps on purpose. He came back to his right senses and panicked. How could he escape the consequences? By blaming Dorothy. Dorothy was young and overworked and worried and perhaps still rather deeply in love with him. At any rate, she did not know then just what he was like. He conceived a masterstroke. Put it into Dorothy's mind that she had been to blame and at the same time Gerry would get rid of his own guilt and have a wonderful hold over Dorothy. And so he persuaded her that the death of the child was entirely her own doing, and she was the more easily persuaded when he very nobly agreed to share the blame himself. She certainly believed him at first. Perhaps she has believed him for a long time. But suppose she no longer believes him? Suppose she is willing to accuse him? Wouldn't you say she was in serious danger? Wouldn't you say that her only protection would be to play along with Gerry and pretend to him that she is still blaming herself? If she is weak and guilty, she is no threat to him. But if she's strongminded enough to bring the whole truth out into the open . . . oh, my God, what have I done!" exclaimed Peter, stopping suddenly in his tracks and staring at Bill Thorn in horror. "Bullying her into telling me!"

"You've probably saved her soul," said Bill quietly.

"I reckon I've signed her death warrant!" cried Peter.

Bill got up and took him by the arm and gently forced him to sit down again. "It's not going to help if we get into a panic ourselves," he said. "You may be right about Dorothy being in danger, but that is nothing new and it is certainly not your doing. She has been in danger from Gerry for years."

"Not as badly as this."

"Not as badly as this, but don't forget that she is not alone with Gerry. Nina and I are here too. I know what you're thinking. An old man and a young girl—what protection can they possibly be against a maniac? They can be a very good protection, my dear Peter, believe me."

"If only she'd come away with me. Or if only I could stay here. I could hide in the garden—"

"It would be most unwise of you to stay on the premises. Look what happened last time. I swear to you, Peter, that I am going to get Dorothy away from Gerry. Not tonight. Tomorrow. I promise you. She will come to no harm tonight. I will keep watch on Gerry upstairs. Nina will keep watch on Dorothy down here."

"But if he gets really violent—"

"He is still no match for the three of us. And he won't get violent. It will be done by subtlety if anything is to be done at all. Peter, you must go now. Please trust me."

But when Peter was at the door Bill called him back again. "I very nearly forgot. Could you show me how to work this gadget of Dorothy's? I want to record a radio programme. I'm afraid I'm a dreadful old duffer at this sort of thing."

The gadget was a little tape-recorder.

"Dorothy has been using it to record interviews with patients for some research she has been doing," said Mr. Thorn. "She always gets their permission, of course, and I know she is very careful to destroy all material that is not going to be used . . . thank you, Peter. Yes, I've got the hang of it now. Good night, my dear boy, and thank you again. I'll be in touch in the morning."

After one last anxious glance at the closed door of the consulting-room, Peter left the house. He had never believed it possible that he could feel this overwhelming urge to take a fellow creature's life. If he were to run into Gerry now he would not be responsible for his actions; there would be no restraining himself. He had to admit that the old man was right to send him away, but it was terribly hard to go. He lingered for a moment or two in the drive, assessing the height of the consulting-room window from the ground and wondering whether to attempt a midnight abduction of Dorothy—willing or unwilling. Why hadn't her father persuaded her to come away now? Surely he would have been able to do so? What was he up to? Why the tape-recorder? Peter didn't believe for a moment that Bill simply wanted to record a radio programme. The old man was playing some deep game of his own, gambling with Dorothy's life.

By the time he had reached the van Peter had worked himself up into a state of great indignation against Dorothy's father. He switched on the engine and the lights and sat staring at the white gateposts of Pond Cottage, as he had done on another occasion not so very long ago. A car came slowly past the van, turned left in front of it, and paused for a moment before proceeding between the gateposts. The driver turned to look at Peter. His face was clearly visible in the remaining light of day, aided by the headlamps and the streetlamp. And Peter's face was equally visible to him.

If he gets out I am going to run him down, thought Peter, putting the van into gear and watching intently.

But Gerry did not get out. He drove on up the drive and round the corner of the house. Peter switched off the engine and the lights again and slumped back dejectedly in his seat. It seemed to him that he had done nothing but harm all round. He had shaken Dorothy out of the listless passivity in which alone she was safe from Gerry; he had not followed his own deep instinct to stay in the house regardless of Mr. Thorn's wishes; and he had not got away in time to conceal his visit from Gerry.

One by one the lights in the windows of Pond Cottage went out, and Peter was still sitting in the van near to the gate. He could neither bring himself to go in nor to drive away. he cursed himself for his own bungling, and was tormented by thoughts of what Gerry might be saying or doing to his wife.

18

"You know it's the only way," said the low voice, very gently, very persuasively. "You can't live with it any longer and it's so easy to end it all . . . easy to end it . . . easy to end it . . ."

Dorothy lay curled up under the bedclothes on the couch in the quiet room. The thick curtains were drawn across and no crack of light showed through them. The door was shut. The still darkness was infinitely soothing. Like the womb, like the tomb. She wanted nothing else; no light, no movement, no struggle. Just for the quiet and the rest and the darkness to go on and on, for the sleep that was on its way to her to last forever.

She didn't know whether the voice was inside her own head or outside it. It felt like inside; it spoke her own thoughts.

"There's water and the bottle there. Within reach on the table. Very little effort. It will only take a few seconds. You've already had two of them. All you have to do is to reach out, empty the rest of them into your hand, lift the glass, lift your head, and swallow. Not much effort to make for everlasting peace. For freedom . . . for peace. Not much to do. It's so easy . . . so easy . . . so easy . . ."

The thoughts were hers and the desire was hers. Only somewhere there seemed to be a stubborn little nagging voice that was pulling in the opposite direction. This other voice was definitely not in herself; it was somewhere outside her, this voice that was so insistently trying to frustrate her own wishes. She wished it would go away, this other nagging voice, and leave her in peace with the thoughts that she wished to hear.

"It's so easy . . . just stretch out your hand . . . empty the bottle . . . so easy . . ."

The low comforting voice went on and on.

"All right," said Dorothy, but whether she said it aloud or only in her own mind she did not know, "I'll do it. I'll do it in a minute . . . I'll do it now."

Her hand reached out, felt the edge of the table, found the bottle. Its lid felt very loose. The feeblest effort would set its contents free.

The comforting voice that spoke her own thoughts went on and on, encouraging her, helping her.

And then the lovely peace was shattered. There came a piercing, intolerable shaft of light; a scream followed by scuffling noises. All was glare and movement and angry voices.

Dorothy curled herself into a tight little ball and pulled the covers over her head. If only it would all go away, leave her in peace to listen to her comforter again, so that she could make just that last little effort.

It went away at last. The still darkness came back, the shouting and the scuffling died except for a distant muffled banging that disturbed her no more than the faint hum of traffic from the main road.

But the comforting voice had gone too.

Dorothy pulled the covers off her head, stretched her limbs, and then curled up again and waited to recapture the drift to endless oblivion.

It would not come.

She was hot and cold and hungry and cramped and the screaming and the scuffling sounds went on and on inside her head. She moved the pillows and shifted her own position, but still there was no rest and no relief. She raised herself on one elbow but felt so giddy that she quickly lay down again. Thoughts and memories and images came in disconnected flashes. There was no clear reasoning; she did not try to work out what the scuffling and the screaming could have meant. Perhaps it had been a dream. Perhaps the comforting voice had been a dream. All she knew was that she was now awake, weak, giddy, feverish, but certainly awake, lying in bed on the ground floor of her own home, and that there was no regaining the lost paradise of nothingness. All the myriad aches and stabs of human consciousness were with her again, and she wept for the peace of death that had been snatched from her.

Mr. Thorn, standing in the darkness just inside the door of his room, waited until the shouting had died down and the slight creak of the bedroom door opposite to his own had come and gone. Then he made his way silently and very slowly down the thick carpeted staircase, holding on to the rail with one hand, and holding a little torch in the other. In the hall he paused for a moment or two to take careful breaths. There was a muffled thumping sound audible down here. It seemed to come from the back of the house, but Bill Thorn moved first to the door of the consulting-room, which was slightly ajar. The torchlight showed Dorothy curled up with her face to the wall and one arm flung outside the bedclothes.

"Are you all right?" asked Mr. Thorn softly.

She stirred slightly and moaned. He could not tell whether she was asleep or not. He felt for the hand and held it a moment. The pulse seemed to be steady, the breathing even. He laid the hand back on the cover and flashed the little torch on to the bedside table. There was a glass of water standing there and near it a bottle nearly full of dark-coloured capsules. Bill thought for a moment and then drew out a handkerchief from the pocket of his dressing-gown, held it lightly round the bottle, and dropped them both into the pocket. Then he switched off the torch and stood still by the side of the couch for a while. Dorothy made no further sound, and her breathing remained steady, but the distant muffled thumping was still going on.

Mr. Thorn came out into the hall. As he neared the kitchen he could hear faint cries for help. He shut the kitchen door behind him, walked across and opened the door that led to a small utility room, and said, "Is that you, Nina? Where are you?"

"In the broom-cupboard," came the stifled reply.

Mr. Thorn turned the key of the broom-cupboard and Nina collapsed at his feet, lay there for a moment, and then picked herself up.

"Dorothy," she cried hoarsely. "Got to see to Dorothy."

And she would have rushed off at once if Mr. Thorn had not restrained her.

"Dorothy is all right. She's asleep. I've just been to look. What happened, Nina?"

"He was by her bed, whispering to her in the dark," replied the girl. "I thought I heard something. I went in and switched on the light. I couldn't get near Dorothy. I didn't even see her. He got hold of me and locked me in here. Are you quite sure she's all right? Hadn't I better go and see?"

It was clear that Nina's anxiety was not to be put at rest.

"Go and see for yourself," said Mr. Thorn. "But don't wake her. Don't go too near her."

After the girl had gone he lowered himself stiffly into a kitchen chair and put a hand on the outside of the dressing-gown pocket. There will be his fingerprints on the bottle, he said to himself, which won't prove anything but it will help a little, because these are Dorothy's sleeping pills and there was no need for him to be handling them. And then there's that little gadget. Bill Thorn glanced at his watch. I'm afraid it won't have anything much on it, because Peter said the tape would only run an hour. But one never knows. It might have picked up something. And Gerry is not to know when it was put in place. Bluff ought to be enough. It will take him by surprise to learn that I had thought of recording him. Even with all his cunning he would never suspect that of me. His highly-respected father-in-law to go bugging a room! Even in his own thoughts the old man used the phrase a little self-consciously. He was indeed very surprised at himself, but having made up his mind, he was going to shirk nothing, absolutely nothing. He had, in the last resort, his own life to give. Those who do not care whether they live or die, they are the strongest, he said to himself.

But Nina must be kept out of it. She was young and had everything to live for. Mr. Thorn had no doubt that the girl would gladly put herself in front of an assassin's gun in order to protect Dorothy, but she must not be allowed to get into such a position. She had suffered enough violence already this evening.

"Well, my dear," he said when Nina returned. "Are you convinced now?"

"I suppose so," said Nina reluctantly. "But what was he doing there, whispering to her in the dark?"

"I don't know," said Mr. Thorn, "but it can't have been anything to upset her. You can see she's come to no harm. Which is more than can be said of you, my poor child."

He looked at the girl with concern. Nina did indeed look very battered and dishevelled.

"Oh, I'm all right," she said impatiently. "I can look after myself. And I'm not going to leave Dorothy alone. I'm going to stay in the consulting-room for the rest of the night. No one can stop me. I won't disturb her. I'll lie on the floor near the door."

This was not quite what Bill Thorn had wanted, but he merely said, "I don't think it is necessary, but if it would make you happier, then you do that. Perhaps you would warm me up some milk first, will you? And I'll look in on Dorothy again while you're doing it."

I don't trust her not to go snooping around, he said to himself as he retrieved the tape-recorder from under the couch. She's much too bright and suspicious. I'll have to think up some means of keeping her out of the way when I tackle Gerry. Shall I do it tonight? No, I think it had better be tomorrow. He isn't likely to come out of his room again tonight. Not after all that rumpus. And having his behaviour to Nina to explain away.

Mr. Thorn placed the little tape-recorder next to the radio in the sitting-room. My fingerprints are all over it, he said to himself, but that does not matter. It's the bottle I have to be careful about. The tape is merely for bluff. And in any case, with any luck this will not be a matter for the police. Not in that way, at any rate.

When he had drunk the warm milk he said to Nina, "I think I will doss down on the settee in the sitting-room for the rest of the night. It's just as comfortable as a bed and I shall do very well there."

Nina looked shocked. "You ought to be in bed, in your state of health."

"Of course I ought." Mr. Thorn smiled. "But I'm not going to. I don't feel at all bad. Do I look as if I'm going to collapse on you again?"

Nina had to own that he did not. In fact, he looked astonishingly spry for an old man who had recently been so ill and had been got out of his bed only a little while after retiring to it.

"I don't think Mr. Laver will disturb us again," said Mr. Thorn. "He will be rather ashamed of himself after losing his head and locking you up like that. If anything does happen, we are within call of each other and of Dorothy."

He stood up, took the girl's hand, and pressed it to his lips. "Thank you with all my heart, my dear little Nina, for being such a good watchdog for my daughter. May God bless you."

The hours of darkness passed in silence. Outside Pond Cottage Peter dozed over the wheel of the van, hoping that Middle Lane was free of nocturnal wandering policemen who might wonder what he was doing there. And inside the house Dorothy stirred again and then once more cried herself to sleep, unaware that three guardian angels were watching over her.

19

When the early summer dawn came, it occurred to Peter
that if he was not going to try to get into the house, it would
be more sensible to be somewhere where Nina could reach
him by telephone. He drove home, made tea, sat down at
the table, opened his copy of Galbraith's *The New Industrial
State*, which was a set book for his course, and stared at it
uncomprehendingly. After an hour of this he shut the book
up in disgust with himself and tried to sleep. By eight he
was at the shop, quite certain that Nina had been trying to
get in touch with him there and that something disastrous
had happened to Dorothy. When Len came in at half past
eight, Peter told him in great agitation that he was expecting
a call any moment on a personal matter and asked Len to be
sure to give the caller the number of the house where he
would be working for the day. The owners had gone on
holiday to escape the upheaval of rewiring and had given
Peter the key and the run of the place.

He was struggling to get the fitted carpet in the dining
room out of the way without doing any damage to it when
the telephone rang. It never occurred to him that it was more
likely to be a call for the owners than for himself, so much

had the affairs of Pond Cottage come to dominate his whole
horizon and upset his normal balance. It was, in fact, Nina
ringing from a call-box.

"Mr. Thorn told me to ring you," she said, "to say to
stay away from here. He says he's got everything under
control and he'll let you know when to come. He wants me
to keep out of the way too, but I'm not going to. I'm going
back. I won't interfere with him but I've got to be there."

"But what's happening?" cried Peter in an agony of
bewilderment. "Hi—don't ring off."

Nina, who appeared to think that her cryptic message
provided an adequate report on events, had seemed about to
do so.

"Here—give me the number of the box," said Peter.
"I'll dial it and you won't have to keep putting coins in."

She gave it and rang off and he dialled and waited in
misery until she answered.

"Is Dorothy all right?" he asked immediately.

"I suppose so, but they don't seem to want her to wake
up properly."

"Who is 'they'?" Peter was irritable and impatient until
it occurred to him that Nina, too, might have had a very bad
night and be feeling confused and afraid. "Do you mean
Mr. Thorn?" he added more gently.

"Yes, and Dr. Ferguson. He sent for him and they sent
me out of the room but I overheard some of it. She's to stay
asleep all morning. I think he's given her an injection of
something. Her mind needs a very long rest, they said."

Nina sounded very worried. Peter made an effort to
console her. "Look, if it's Dr. Ferguson and her father, it
must be all right. She was terribly tired, wasn't she, and
couldn't rest properly. I don't suppose she's had a good
night's sleep for months."

"I suppose that's all it is, but I wish they'd let me talk to
her. I wish I knew what they were doing."

"So do I," groaned Peter.

"I wish she was having this rest somewhere else."

"Me too. But I don't see how she can come to any harm, honestly. Dr. Ferguson wouldn't allow it. What's Gerry Laver doing?"

"After he locked me in the broom-cupboard last night," began Nina.

"Locked you in the broom-cupboard!" exclaimed Peter, with all his anxieties returning in full force.

Nina gave a hasty account of the events of the night as far as she knew them. "What was he doing there, whispering to her in the dark?" she demanded as she had done of Mr. Thorn. Peter's mind only went as far as subliminal suggestion or "sleep learning," which he had been reading about recently with a view to trying to speed up his studies.

"What's he like this morning?" he asked. "Gerry Laver, I mean."

"Sort of funny. Doesn't say much. Looks sort of trapped. But nasty too."

Peter didn't find this sketchy description at all comforting. A kind of simmering viciousness was all too characteristic of Gerry. But surely he couldn't actually do Dorothy any harm, not if she was lying there unconscious. Or could he? Presumably he could use a hypodermic and had access to drugs. Peter groaned again. What the hell was going on in that house? What was Bill Thorn up to?

He asked this last question aloud.

"Mr. Thorn said he was going to talk to him seriously," replied Nina, "and that no one was to interrupt. I don't like it."

"Neither do I," said Peter.

"He'll kill the old man."

"Oh no. I don't think so." Belatedly Peter realized again how much Nina herself needed comforting. "Mr. Thorn can look after himself. But it might bring on another of his attacks. That's what is so worrying. I don't see how you can do anything to stop it, though."

"I've got to go," said Nina abruptly, and rang off, leaving Peter staring stupidly at his customer's telephone and wondering whether he ought to leave some money for the call.

Nina ran up the road from the call-box and in at the front door of Pond Cottage. Then she tiptoed into the consulting-room. It was cool and quiet and dim in there, with the curtains drawn against the morning sun. Nina stood looking down at Dorothy. They had said she was perfectly all right and only needed a very long sleep, but she looked very white and her breathing seemed scarcely to stir the bedcover. Nina could not help being afraid. She longed to put her arms around Dorothy and beg her not to desert her, to come back to life, but she dared not. Instead she stood twisting her hands together in unconscious imitation of Dorothy's own habitual gesture of tension and whispered her plea.

"Please get well, please get well. Don't go and leave me all alone again."

Then she ran to the door of Gerry's study and put her ear to the keyhole. She would hear if there was any sound of a fight. If he hit the old man she was going to go in and do something about it: kick him where it hurt most. She would get it in first this time instead of being bundled ignominiously into the broom-cupboard.

But there was no sound of any violence, nor indeed of any movement at all from within the room. There was nothing but the old man's voice going on and on. Nina could hear it perfectly clearly.

"I am not condemning you," he said. "No one of us has any right to condemn another. And I realize that yours is a sickness of the mind rather than a crime. But the suffering it has caused has got to come to an end. It killed your own daughter—"

There was a pause, in which Nina, rapidly digesting this statement, could hear no sound from either of the two men in the room.

"—and last night it nearly killed mine," continued the voice of Mr. Thorn. "Last night you made a deliberate attempt to induce Dorothy to kill herself by taking an excessive dose of her sleeping capsules. Dorothy is not a child whom you can easily induce to swallow a fatal dose when one of your mad fits of jealousy comes upon you. She would not ignorantly swallow a poison—at any rate not any poison known to chemistry. But you have been poisoning her nevertheless. Poisoning her mind for many years, persuading her that in a tragic moment when her own mind was overburdened with its responsibilities, she made a mistake and gave the wrong dosage to her own child.''

For a moment the old man's voice seemed to falter and then it went on again, more strongly than before. ''That is in the past. It is last night with which we are concerned at this moment. This is a very different matter. I have firm evidence of attempted murder. When Dorothy was totally exhausted in mind and body and longing only for rest you worked upon her to push her over the edge and you put the means of self-destruction within her grasp.''

''Well, well.'' Gerry spoke at last. ''I never could have thought you capable of inventing such a curious story, Bill. However. Do go on. I am all agog to hear the end.''

The tones were as mocking as ever, but Nina believed she could detect some anxiety as well.

''I am not bluffing, I assure you,'' continued Mr. Thorn. ''I have evidence enough to warrant a police enquiry, at any rate.''

''Evidence! Come now, Bill aren't you being just a teeny bit fanciful?''

''The bottle bearing your fingerprints, with the lid left very loose so that it would be easy for Dorothy to open it, is now locked up safely in Dr. Ferguson's possession. The tape-recording of your voice—''

''Tape-recording?'' Nina, feeling her own heart give a sudden jump, could almost hear Gerry's start from the other side of the closed door.

''Tape-recording,'' repeated Mr. Thorn firmly. ''This too is in safety—in possession of Dr. Ferguson. It is not very clear, but it is none the less unmistakably your own voice. There will be witnesses to swear to that, I think."

Gerry laughed, but not very convincingly. "Really, Bill, this is too absurd. You don't know how to use a tape-recorder. You've often said so. And in any case a tape doesn't run for long."

"I admit that I know very little about these electrical gadgets myself," said Mr. Thorn, "and that is why I consulted an expert."

"An expert?" Again there was a quick change in Gerry's voice and Nina heard the sound of movement in the room. "An expert! That man!" There was menace in the voice now. "He was here. I saw him. You've been plotting together. You'll pay for this."

There came further sounds. Nina gripped the doorhandle and drew a deep breath to prepare herself for the attack. But almost instantly her own grip relaxed. Mr. Thorn's voice sounded as steady as ever and it seemed that he still had the situation well under control.

"If you make any attempt on my life or injure me in any way," he said, "that is certainly the end as far as you are concerned. And it won't be treatment in a mental hospital that I am proposing for you. It will be a prison sentence. If that is what you want, then go ahead. It is of no great consequence to me. I am old and sick and have not much longer to live in any case."

After this there was a silence, lasting what seemed to Nina for a very long time. She held her breath. Then Mr. Thorn said, "I don't know whether your form of sickness of the mind can be cured. Science is able to do a lot nowadays, and it may be that you can be helped. I hope so. I would like at any rate to give you the chance to try to heal yourself. I have been making enquiries and have made provisional arrangements for you to be taken into hospital at once."

He paused once more and Nina thought she could hear some muttering sounds, but could distinguish no words.

"I have been able to do this," went on Mr. Thorn,

"without actually mentioning your attempt to kill Dorothy. This need not be made public and the evidence can remain unused provided you keep to certain conditions. They are two in number and very simple."

The old man was speaking as calmly as ever. There was no malice in his voice; there might even have been a touch of compassion, but there was a quiet ruthlessness about it that made Nina shiver.

"The first condition is that you do not try to leave the hospital or communicate with Dorothy in any way. The second is that you relieve Dorothy once and for all of her undeserved feelings of guilt about Irene by signing a statement that you were solely responsible for the death of the child. I have prepared such a document for you to sign. I do not call it a confession, because that implies free will, and I do not think you were responsible for your actions when you gave that overdose to Irene. I believe that you were out of your mind. You will see that I have not written that it was done deliberately. That is not necessary for Dorothy's peace of mind. It is enough that she knows it was not her doing. After she has read the statement it will be destroyed. Nobody else will ever know of its existence. It is up to you, if you wish, before you sign it to add a rider asking her forgiveness. But the evidence of your last night's attempt will not be destroyed. It will be used if you refuse to sign this statement or if, having signed it, you refuse to remain in hospital. I will leave it with you now. I have another copy if this one should become damaged."

Nina pressed her head more closely to the door. Again she thought she had heard Gerry say something, but could not hear what it was.

"It may be," said Mr. Thorn, and it seemed to Nina that his voice was at last beginning to show signs of tiring, "that you will decide not to sign because you have some other plan of escape in your mind. I will not try to guess what that plan is. I will not try to frustrate your plan provided it causes no harm to Dorothy. It will be advisable, however, to come to a decision within the next few hours."

After that came the distinct sound of a chair being moved back and Nina hastily retreated a couple of yards. The door of the study began to open and Nina made a dash for the kitchen. When Mr. Thorn came in a few minutes later she was rushing about opening and shutting drawers and cupboards in a meaningless manner. If he suspected that she had been eavesdropping, he gave no sign of it.

"This is the key to the consulting-room," he said. "I have taken the precaution of locking the door. There is very little likelihood that my daughter will wake for several hours yet, but I'd like you to keep this safe and go in every now and then to see how she is. Will you do that, please, Nina?"

"Yes," said Nina taking the key and putting it into the pocket of her jeans. "I'll keep it on me."

She glanced up at him apprehensively. He looked just the same as before: an old man whom she had surprisingly come to like and respect, although normally she didn't have much use for old people. He talked in an interesting way and treated you as if you were interesting too. She felt that they were friends, but she would not have expected him to be a force to be reckoned with. After all, he was only a sick old man, and as such was to be cared for or put up with, according to your tastes. It was very difficult to picture him as the owner of the voice that she had heard from the other side of the study door—the voice of retribution. She was longing to ask him about Mr. Laver but was afraid to do so. She would be sure to give away the fact that she had been eavesdropping at the door, and then the old man would talk to her in that awful way and she could not bear it.

"Are you all right?" she asked instead.

Mr. Thorn smiled in his usual manner and Nina felt a little better.

"You are surprised that I'm not in a state of total collapse," he said. "I'll let you into a secret. I am pepped up—is that the phrase?—with some sort of wonder drug that keeps you going during an emergency. You'll probably know more about it than I do. Dr. Ferguson was reluctant, but I explained how important it was that I should keep my strength up for the next few hours, and in the end he allowed himself to be persuaded. The effects will wear off later on and I shall become very feeble, and you will have to be very patient with me again. But I hope that by then we shall see more clearly what is to happen."

"What is going to happen?" asked Nina in a frightened whisper.

"I don't know, my dear. It's in the lap of the gods. We must try to be patient."

"Shall I—" Nina broke off and then took the plunge, "Shall I get Mr. Laver some lunch?"

Mr. Thorn considered the question. "No, I think not," he said at last. "Have you got any leftovers in the 'fridge that he can come and get if he wants to?"

Nina reeled off an impressive list of cold meats and cheeses and various other delicacies.

"Then we'll leave it at that," said Mr. Thorn. "I'm afraid I don't feel very hungry myself. This pep pill, perhaps. Or some other reason. But a cup of tea later on would be very welcome. I shall be in the sitting-room. I don't feel in quite the right mood for the garden. Do you know where the papers have got to?"

Nina found him the two daily papers that came into the house and he smiled and thanked her and settled down to read, just as if he were any other harmless and kindly old gentleman who had nothing more in his mind than the news of the day and where to go for his walk and what was for dinner.

When Nina came out of the sitting-room she heard a door close on the floor above. There was no wind that day, and with Dorothy lying dead to the world and Mr. Thorn sitting on the settee reading there was only one person who could have closed it. She ran back to Mr. Thorn and cried in an excited whisper: "He's gone upstairs!"

"Well, what of it?" He looked at her in mild reproach above his reading glasses. "A man may move around his own house, mayn't he?"

"I thought you'd like to know," said Nina.

Mr. Thorn's look became rather more severe. "Nina," he said, "have you been—"

But Nina had vanished, guessing what he was going to ask her.

— 20 —

Nina looked in on Dorothy, saw that all was well, and then went to the kitchen and tried to amuse herself by planning meals, but without much success. She could not even keep still. Her mind was in a turmoil, going over and over the amazing things that she had overheard. Dorothy's baby, and Gerry trying to kill Dorothy, and Mr. Thorn threatening Gerry . . . She came out into the hall and stood listening, she did not know for what. Then, becoming very bold, she opened the door of Gerry's study and peeped inside. As she had expected, there was nobody there, and she tiptoed over to the desk. The urge to find out whether the "confession" was lying there and if so, whether he had signed it, was irresistible.

There was no sheet of paper lying on the blotter; only the ballpoint pen that Gerry normally used. Nina leafed through a couple of books and an educational journal that were lying on the desk and then glanced around the room. If he had signed it and put it into a book or into a drawer she would have a long search. Perhaps it was in the wastepaper basket. She squatted on the floor and examined the contents. A few used envelopes, that was all. The sound of running water in

145

the house caused Nina to leap to her feet and stand
quivering for a moment behind the study door. Then, drawn
back as if by a magnet to the desk, she bent more closely
over the blotter. The pressure of a ballpoint, used on a
single sheet of paper, would surely leave a mark on the
blotter underneath. The blotting-paper was barely used:
Gerry was fastidious about taking a clean sheet every
morning, whether or not he intended to do any writing that
day. In the right-hand bottom corner Nina believed she
could discern the faint imprint of a signature: Gerard F.
Laver. Of course this did not necessarily mean he had
signed the confession: he might have been putting his name
to some quite unimportant document for all she knew. But it
was exciting to find this, all the same. And even more
exciting when she believed she could distinguish some
further marks underneath the signature, right at the lower
edge of the blotter. These were less clear, however. She
could make out a few letters, but no full word.

Nina stood up again and wondered what to do now. If
Gerry had indeed signed the paper, then Mr. Thorn ought to
know at once. But how could Nina convey her information
to Mr. Thorn without letting on that she had been eaves
dropping? How could she persuade the old man to go into
the study? She stood by the desk, grimacing at the blotter,
and for a moment she almost wished she had not listened in
to the conversation at all, so great was the burden of the
knowledge she had gained thereby, so overwhelming was
her need to talk to somebody about it all. She thought of
Peter, but was not sure whether he, too, might not blame
her. In any case, she dared not telephone him from the
house and she could not leave the house because it was her
job to keep an eye on Dorothy.

As she stood here in increasingly agitated indecision, she
once again heard the sound of running water. Somebody
was using the downstairs cloakroom. Probably Mr. Thorn.
Terrified that he might step across the hall and find her in the
study, Nina rushed out and along to the sitting-room. Mr.
Thorn was not there. He had evidently finished with the

newspapers because they were lying folded on the coffee-table, and on top of them lay an open book. Nina picked it up. It had a pale green jacket similar to those on a row of books on one of the shelves in Dorothy's consulting-room. What's he reading medical books for, wondered Nina, and then she looked at the title: *Self-poisoning: an Investigation into Cases Treated in a Special Unit.*

Self-poisoning, muttered Nina to herself; I could tell them something about that. And so could Gerry Laver. She was about to replace the book on the table, open as she had found it, when a few words caught her eye. "This widely used and convenient household remedy is by no means without its dangers, and if the patient fails to vomit within—"

That was all Nina had time to take in. She had put the book back and was puffing up the cushions on the settee when Mr. Thorn came back into the room.

"Would you like your tea now?" asked Nina in the most innocent of voices.

"Not just yet, thank you," said Mr. Thorn. "In about half an hour's time, if that is convenient to you."

"All right."

Mr. Thorn settled himself comfortably on the settee and picked up his book.

"Do you think it would be all right if I go and dust the study now?" asked Nina.

Mr. Thorn looked up and said severely: "Have you any particular reason for wanting to do it at this moment?"

"I just thought of it," muttered Nina lamely, and once more she fled from the room and took refuge in the kitchen. All sorts of ideas were beginning to boil up in her mind, and for all her histrionic powers, she did not feel able to be with Mr. Thorn in the same room without giving some of them away. Could it possibly be true, what she was beginning to suspect of him? Was it possible that this nice kindly old man could look just the same as ever and chat about cups of tea while all the time he was relentlessly pushing another human being into suicide? For Nina could not help but feel that this was Mr. Thorn's intention. This must be the "other plan for escape" that he had mentioned to Gerry, the plan that he himself would not frustrate provided it did not harm Dorothy. In other words, if Gerry chose to kill himself rather than go to hospital or have his murderous attempt on Dorothy made public, then Mr. Thorn would not stop him. And Dorothy, who might yet try to save his life in spite of everything, was to be kept out of action until it was all over.

It was appalling to think that this was in the old man's mind, but Nina could see no other explanation for his behaviour. The only thing that didn't quite seem to fit was the book that he was reading. Self-poisoning cases. People who had swallowed overdoses of drugs. He would obviously be interested in this if that was his plan for Gerry, but on the other hand why should he be reading about first-aid methods? That rather looked as if he was thinking of trying to save Gerry's life after all.

Nina, who had been sitting huddled up on the kitchen stool, suddenly got to her feet and cried aloud, "What shall I do? Oh, whatever shall I do? Ought I to tell Mr. Thorn I know about it and beg him to stop Gerry killing himself . . . ought I to try to stop him myself . . . ought I to wake Dorothy . . ."

She began to run around the kitchen, beating her hands against her head. Suppose Gerry had gone upstairs to take his own life. She hated him; she wished him dead, but all the same . . . You couldn't be in the same house with someone trying to kill himself and not do anything about it. Or could you? It was plain enough that Mr. Thorn could do just that. Why, it was scarcely better than murder . . . an old man like that, a clergyman, a man who cared so much about other people and was so tolerant and so willing to forgive everything . . .

Fragments of one of the many discussions she had had with him came back to Nina's mind. They had been talking about the sacredness of life—plant, human and animal. "Yes, I would shoot a rabid dog," Mr. Thorn had said. "It is sad, because it is not the animal's fault, but it has to be done to protect others."

"And if it's a human being who is running wild?" Nina had asked.

"The same applies," he had answered. "Although of course one should make every possible effort to render him harmless in some other way before taking such drastic action."

Presumably, thought Nina, Mr. Thorn thought of Gerry Laver as a rabid dog or a lunatic at large with a knife. She supposed that most people would agree that other people had to be protected. She'd agreed with it herself during their discussion. But to take the law into one's own hands like that . . . wasn't that a bit different?

Nina sat down on the stool again and covered her face with her hands.

"If only I didn't know anything about it," she moaned. With all her heart she wished now that she had never listened at the study door, never seen what Mr. Thorn was reading. It was a terrible thing to feel that you might have the responsibility for life or death in your hands.

Suddenly she could bear it no longer. If she were out of the house it would be less her responsibility. Even in the garden she would not feel quite so close to it. Ashamed of herself for her own cowardice, quite forgetting that she was supposed to be making tea, she gave way to the impulse to run away and hide until it was all over, whatever "it" might be.

At the side of the house where the old coachhouse, now the garage, stood, there was a little shrubbery. Nina made her way there, sat down on the grass under a lilac bush, and hugged her knees. Then she tried to beat her mind into forgetfulness by repeating the same sentence over and over again. This method had sometimes worked in the past when she had been caught up in something terrifying that she didn't know how to cope with. It's nothing to do with you, she told herself, and went on telling herself this for a long time.

After a while she thought she would be more comfortable if she lay down, and she stretched herself out on the grass, still repeating her sentence. It began to have a hypnotic effect. She had had a sleepless night and many hours of great tension and anxiety. Her hands relaxed and the words of the sentence began to get jumbled up and then stopped coming altogether.

When Nina woke the sun had gone off the bushes and she was stiff and shivery. Her first thought was horror that she had forgotten to check whether Dorothy was all right. She fished for the key to the consulting-room and ran back into the house. All was exactly as she had left it. Dorothy was still asleep, Mr. Thorn was still reading in the sitting-room and did not even look up when Nina put her head round the door. And there was still no sign of Gerry. It was as if time had stopped while she slept. But the hands of the clock had moved on. The electric clock over the kitchen door said half past three.

I can't bear it any longer, said Nina to herself: I don't care what happens. I shall have to go upstairs to see.

It was when she reached the foot of the stairs that she heard the first faint groaning sounds. At first she thought it must be Dorothy, and hastily she unlocked the consulting-room door again and crept inside.

"Are you all right?" she whispered.

Dorothy woke, muttered something, and turned over again as if she was wanting to go back to sleep. She was not in any distress; the groans could not have come from her. Nina left the room, omitting this time to lock the door behind her. As she stood in the hall she heard the groaning again. She rushed into the sitting-room and caught hold of Mr. Thorn by the arm.

"Please, please, we've got to do something. I can hear him. It's awful. Please can't we *do* something!"

Mr. Thorn got to his feet. "What is it, Nina? What do you want me to do?"

"Go and see if he's all right. It's awful. I can't bear it. He must be ill."

Mr. Thorn looked at her with pity. Nina looked almost more dishevelled and distraught than she had when she fell out of the broom-cupboard.

"All right," he said. "I will go up and see. Wait here."

After what seemed another age she heard his voice again. "Nina."

He was standing at the turn of the stairs, calling her softly. She ran up towards him.

"Will you go and fetch a glass of warm water with salt in it—plenty of salt."

"Salt water?" repeated Nina in a dazed manner.

"Yes. It's a quick way to rid the stomach of poison. I'll wait here for you."

Nina returned with the glass. Her hand was trembling so much that the water slopped over as she carried it.

"Thank you," said Mr. Thorn, taking it from her.

"Hadn't we better . . ." began Nina.

"Yes?" He turned to face her again.

"Hadn't we better phone Dr. Ferguson?" she faltered.

Mr. Thorn considered this for a moment. "I doubt if there is any need for it," he said eventually. "And in any case I imagine Dr. Ferguson is out on his rounds. But if you wish you may telephone his surgery and leave a message. Say that Mr. Laver has swallowed four or five sleeping tablets and is still conscious and that I am giving warm salt water as an emetic. Will you give that message to the receptionist, please, Nina?"

"Yes," said Nina softly.

She telephoned the surgery. Dr. Ferguson was not there. She repeated the message and the receptionist promised to contact the doctor as soon as possible.

"Is it—is it all right giving him salt water?" asked Nina.

"Oh yes." The voice at the other end was brisk and confident. "That's the standard first-aid treatment when the patient is still conscious. Once he's brought up the poison he'll be better."

"But you will tell Dr. Ferguson, won't you, as soon as you can?" begged Nina.

The voice promised that it would. Nina replaced the receiver, feeling only partially reassured. She would much rather have spoken to the elderly Scots doctor herself. He, at any rate, could be trusted not to do anything really wrong.

She ran upstairs and stood still on the half landing. There were sounds coming from the bedroom. She felt that she ought to go in but her feet would not take her. Mr. Thorn heard her and came out. She reported her conversation with the doctor's receptionist. Mr. Thorn made no comment, but handed her the empty glass. "Some more," he said. "It's not working yet."

Nina fetched another glass of warm salt water and then another.

"Hasn't he been sick?" she whispered to Mr. Thorn as she handed over the glass at the bedroom door.

The old man moved his head slowly from side to side before going back into the bedroom. Nina stood outside on the landing. The sentence she had read in the book on self-poisoning seemed to be burning itself into her mind.

"This widely used and convenient household remedy is not without its dangers, and if the patient does not quickly vomit . . ."

It was no good. She could not bear it any longer. She would have to go and find the book and read the rest of that sentence. And suppose it is to do with salt water, she asked herself as she ran downstairs, and suppose it says it is dangerous. What are you going to do then? Tell Mr. Thorn to stop? Refuse to fetch any more? Go and wake Dorothy?

She found the book and the sentence, and was reading the relevant passage with increasing certainty and horror when the front doorbell rang. Nina did not answer it immediately: she was quickly coming to a resolution. It was her own fault that she knew what Mr. Thorn was up to, and she was going to be punished for her eavesdropping by having to live with the knowledge for ever afterwards. Well, she would just have to endure it. She would have to live with her own conscience for always because she knew she could never give him away. Now that she knew for sure she would keep the secret and back him up, whatever happened. Just so long as Dorothy was not suspected. If Dorothy were to be suspected . . . but the last thing in the world that Mr. Thorn would want was that. If Dorothy were suspected then he would certainly come forward to take the blame himself.

The bell rang again, loudly and impatiently. Nina reached the front door at the same time as Dorothy came out of the consulting-room in her nightgown, dazed with sleep.

"What's happening? What's the time?" she asked in a blurred voice.

Nina gave her a despairing look and the front doorbell rang yet again.

"All right, all right," muttered Nina and pulled it open.

A short, plump, fair, well-dressed woman stood on the doorstep. She was red in the face and looked both anxious and bad-tempered.

"What on earth's going on here!" she exclaimed. And then with a little scream, "Dolly! What's the matter with you?"

Dorothy had collapsed on to the chair that stood by the telephone table. "Pauline," she said faintly. "What are you doing here?"

"Doing here?" The newcomer sounded increasingly indignant and alarmed. "What am I doing here? I'm here because Gerry invited me. Didn't he tell you? He said you were feeling rather low and suggested I should come round at tea-time and stay the rest of the evening. I was rather under the impression that I might be able to be of some use. But he didn't tell me you were seriously ill. Hadn't you better be in bed?"

"I've been in bed. It's time I woke up," said Dorothy. She stood up, staggered a step or two forward, and then said weakly: "It's no good. I'll have to go back. Nina, would you look after Pauline? Mrs. Crofts. Get her some tea or something. Where's Gerry?"

"He's upstairs, he's ill!" cried Nina. "I keep trying to tell you." She had in fact been making efforts to whisper into Dorothy's ear without the visitor hearing, but Dorothy was not in a fit state to take notice of hints.

"Ill!" exclaimed Pauline. "He wasn't ill last night. What's the matter with him? What have you been doing?" And she glared at Dorothy. "Why didn't you tell me before?" she demanded suspiciously.

"She didn't know," cried Nina in a fury. "She's been asleep all day and only just woken up."

Pauline took a deep breath and rolled her eyes upwards before speaking. "It looks to me as if you need someone responsible to take charge here," she said. "You—whatever your name is." And she turned to Nina. "You'd better help Dr. Laver back to bed and I'll go upstairs and see what I can do for Mr. Laver. I suppose no one has thought to send for a doctor?"

And she ran upstairs, still talking. Nina stared after her and breathed deeply and rolled her eyes just as Pauline had done. Then she turned to Dorothy.

"I must pull myself together," said Dorothy. "I'll be all right in a minute . . . if you'd get my slippers and dressing-gown . . . thanks, Nina . . . and make some tea. Strong."

Clinging to Nina's arm, she walked to the kitchen and sat down again. "God, my head," she groaned, holding it between her hands as if that was the only way to keep it in its place. "It's splitting. What's the matter with Gerry?"

"I think he's swallowed . . ." began Nina as she switched on the electric kettle.

She was interrupted by the door of the kitchen being flung open. Pauline stood there holding an empty glass. "Salt water!" she cried as she handed the glass to Nina with a dramatic gesture. "Hurry up, girl! It's a matter of life or death."

21

After Pauline had left the room with the replenished glass, Dorothy said to Nina, "What's he done this time?"

She was still holding her head between her hands and looked on the point of collapse again.

"He's swallowed too many sleeping pills," said Nina. "Your father is looking after him, and we've rung Dr. Ferguson's surgery. He's coming as soon as he can."

"Again," muttered Dorothy. "All that over again." She leant forward and beat her head against the kitchen table. "No, no, no," she moaned.

Nina poured boiling water on to the tea-leaves. While Dorothy drank she put an arm round her protectively.

"Thanks," said Dorothy. "I feel better now. Honestly. I'll go up and see what's happening."

At the foot of the stairs she was nearly knocked over by Pauline coming down in a frantic rush.

"He's worse! He's dying!" screamed Pauline. "I'm phoning another doctor."

Dorothy recovered her balance and went slowly upstairs, ignoring Pauline. Pauline turned over pages of the telephone directory, muttering to herself, and Nina, after a moment's uncertainty, followed Dorothy upstairs.

In the big bedroom Gerry lay motionless with his eyes closed. Leaning back in an armchair and looking very white and exhausted sat Mr. Thorn. Dorothy went first to him. "Dad! Are you all right?" she asked anxiously.

He lifted his head and spoke faintly. "Perfectly, my love. But I must rest now. I can't do any more."

"No indeed. You've done more than enough already."

Dorothy turned her attention to Gerry, examined him closely, looked at the bowl that had been put for him to use. She frowned and turned back to her father.

"Has he brought anything up?" she asked.

"No," he murmured. "Not yet."

"How much salt water has he had?"

"I don't know. Quite a lot."

"Five glasses full," said Nina coming forward from the doorway where she had been hovering and looking down on Gerry with fear.

"Five glasses full!" repeated Dorothy in a voice full of alarm. "We must get him to hospital at once. I'll phone for an ambulance."

She picked up the receiver on the bedside telephone extension. Pauline's loud voice, arguing with a doctor's receptionist, became instantly audible.

Dorothy cut in. "Will you clear the line, please. I want to get an ambulance."

"Get off the line!" shouted Pauline. "I'm dealing with this!"

"Make up your minds," snapped the receptionist and replaced the receiver at her end.

"Please let me use the phone, Pauline," said Dorothy in a very strained voice. "This is urgent."

"You're darn right it's urgent. Too urgent to trust you with. Get off!"

Dorothy put down the bedside extension in despair and looked around for Nina. But Nina had gone. Dorothy came downstairs to find her having a tug-of-war with Pauline over the telephone in the hall.

"Nina," said Dorothy. "Leave it alone."

Reluctantly Nina abandoned the struggle, leaving Pauline holding the receiver with both hands.

"I've got to get Gerry to hospital," said Dorothy with weary patience. "If we don't get him in soon he could be dead."

"Dead!" shrieked Pauline. "That's what you want, isn't it? You want him to die—he told me so himself. You've killed him!"

"Shut up, you bloody old cow!" yelled Nina, beside herself with fury.

"Nina," said Dorothy sharply, "will you go to the callbox and dial emergency and ask for an ambulance? Give the address, then my name and title, and tell them I say it's very urgent."

Nina rushed off obediently. Pauline stood clasping the telephone to her as if it were her most treasured possession. Dorothy passed her tongue over her lips as if preparing to speak, but said nothing, and after standing in silence for a moment she returned upstairs, leaving Pauline looking down at the telephone in her hand in a bemused manner.

"I wonder if I ought to go and look," she muttered to herself.

Then she replaced the receiver, gave herself a little shake, and appeared to come to a decision. Dorothy was unlikely to come down again until the ambulance arrived and the girl would be gone for several minutes so there would just be time.

"If anything should happen to me, Pauline," Gerry had said over dinner the previous evening, "I'd like you to have a look inside the folder in the bottom right-hand drawer of my desk if you get the opportunity."

That had been all, but they had been talking about Dorothy and how peculiarly she was behaving, as if she wanted to get rid of Gerry. Hints had been dropped about another man. Pauline had to admit that it looked at the moment as if Dorothy was doing all she could to save Gerry's life, but all the same . . .

After a quick glance around to make quite sure that she was alone on the ground floor of the house, Pauline walked in a purposeful manner towards the study.

When Nina returned from her telephoning Pauline was nowhere to be seen, and if either Nina or Dorothy thought about her at all during the next hour, it was only to be thankful that she had taken herself out of the way. Mr. Thorn was put to bed in his own room; Gerry was put into the ambulance and Dorothy followed in the car. In no time at all, so it seemed to Nina, she was back again.

"He died on the way," she said in almost casual tones, and went straight upstairs to her father.

Nina, left standing alone in the hall, was suddenly overwhelmed by a terrible feeling of desolation.

It's all over, she said to herself; Dorothy doesn't need me any more; she only needs her father. And he doesn't need me either.

After all the tension and excitement and strain the sense of anti-climax was intolerable. In all her lonely life, Nina had never felt quite so lonely before. Dorothy and her father would be consoling each other. There was no place for Nina; she was left out yet again.

But I know what the old man has done, she said to herself: I've got a hold over them. They'll have to keep me here. For a little while fear and resentment struggled with her love and gratitude. And then Dorothy came downstairs and put an arm round her.

"My father wants to see you," she said. Her head drooped low over the girl's shoulder. "He'll never get over this," she added wretchedly.

Nina flung her arms round Dorothy and hugged her. All the desolation and the bitterness and the fear had vanished in a second. She was not going to be turned out. She was needed as much as ever.

"I'll get him well for you," she said. "I did last time, didn't I? You'll see."

And she ran upstairs.

Mr. Thorn was propped up high to ease his breathing. His eyes were closed and he lay white and still. Outwardly he looked just the same as he had looked half an hour ago, when Nina had left him to run downstairs to greet Dorothy. And yet Nina could sense the difference. He had decided to give up the struggle now. He was not going to make any more effort.

"Come," said the old man raising one hand very slightly. "Come and sit by me."

Nina did so. His hand felt for hers and held it. It was he who was giving out strength and comfort to Nina; not Nina to him.

"You have taken a terrible burden of knowledge upon yourself," he said presently. "And you will have to live with it all your life."

Nina could not speak.

"I do not blame you. You were very tempted. Like Eve, perhaps." And the faintest of smiles came over the old man's face.

Nina gave a sob.

"And without you things might have been very different," he went on. "So I have no right to scold."

"I'm sorry," muttered Nina. "I only listened at the door because I was afraid he might hurt you. Truly."

"I believe you, child."

"But the book," went on Nina. "I looked at the book because I had to know."

"Yes, my dear, we will say no more." Mr. Thorn was silent for a little while, conserving his strength. "I am worried for you," he said by and by. "That is why I have mentioned it. Dorothy has no suspicion at all. She need never know anything."

"I'll never, never—" began Nina fervently.

"You will be very tempted," broke in Mr. Thorn, "if you

are ever angry with Dorothy and want to score over her. You see, I hope you will be lifelong friends, but it will be very hard for you, holding such a secret. Will you promise me something, Nina?''

"I can keep secrets," she said.

"Indeed you can. Admirably. But that's not the promise. It is this. If the burden becomes too great for you, if you are ever tempted to use your knowledge to hurt Dorothy, then promise me you will tell Peter and nobody else.''

"I promise," said Nina.

"Thank you." The old man lay back with a little sigh of relief. But a moment later he said, "Don't go yet. There is something else. Let me catch my breath a little.''

Nina got up and began to prepare the oxygen, but he shook his head. "Not necessary. Just a minute or two.''

She sat down again.

"I'm worried about that statement I wrote out for him to sign," said Mr. Thorn after a little while.

Nina interrupted to mention the marks on the blotter.

"Yes. He signed it. I gathered that when I was attending to him. But he wrote something else too—something harmful to Dorothy.''

"Oh no!"

"Oh yes. He could not bear that she should feel free of guilt. You must find that paper before she does, Nina, and use your judgement about whether to show it to her. Or ask Peter.''

"But where is it?''

"Somewhere in the study. You will have to look for it, Nina. I have not had the opportunity or the strength, and it is too late now. Thank you, Nina.''

It was said quietly and calmly and without any particular sign of strain. Nina was silent, expecting him to say something more. To give her a further clue, perhaps, or to say that he was too tired to talk any longer tonight, or to ask her to fetch Dorothy.

But he said nothing more. For a minute or two she

believed he was resting again and she was not unduly concerned. Then a suspicion came into her mind and she stood up and leant over him.

"Oh no, no, no!"

It was a stifled cry. She dropped down on to her knees, caught his hand and began to kiss it again and again, desperately, yearningly.

"You can't leave us—you can't leave us like this," she cried between sobs. "Not without seeing Dorothy again—not without speaking to her. You mustn't go—you mustn't go!"

There was no response from the still figure on the bed. Nina put his hand back on the bedspread and stood up. A moment later Dorothy came into the room and Nina turned on her a face streaming with tears. They clung together for a moment and then, holding hands, looked together down at the bed. William Thorn lay there as still as a marble effigy on a tomb; on his face was an expression of utter contentment and peace.

"Please, Nina," said Dorothy in a strained voice. "Will you do something for me? Peter will be coming soon. He was very anxious to see us all and I couldn't stop him. But I can't see him now. I must stay here. Will you explain to him when he comes? Tell him everything he wants to know."

"Yes," said Nina faintly.

"Thank you, Nina," said Dorothy.

It was said in much the same tones as Mr. Thorn had spoken his last words. With a little cry of distress the girl ran from the room. Peter, arriving shortly afterwards and expecting to have the not unwelcome task of comforting and supporting Dorothy, was confronted instead by a sixteen-year-old girl whom he could see at a glance was at the very end of her strength.

"Nina! What's happened? Where's Dorothy?"

For a nightmarish moment he believed that he was going to hear that Gerry's death had in some extraordinary way deprived Dorothy of her own sanity; that she had after all taken her own life.

"She's all right," gasped Nina. "She said to tell you she's sorry—she can't come—down now."

"She's not ill?" Peter's anxiety receded but did not entirely disappear.

"No. It's Mr. Thorn. He's dead."

Nina blurted it out and then burst into great hiccuping sobs. Automatically Peter put an arm round her. When she was a little calmer she was able to explain in more detail what had happened. Peter listened in a state of grief and shock not so very much different from Nina's own. But even while he was saying that naturally Dorothy wouldn't want to see him or anybody else just now, the chilly certainty was creeping over him that Dorothy was never to be his. She had turned to him in her hour of great bewilderment and fear, but she had not turned to him in her hour of grief. It was an omen: they would be friends and that was all.

So while Nina wept on his shoulder and Peter murmured soothing words, both of them were following up their own thoughts. When Peter said, "It's a wonderful way to die, quickly and easily like that," and Nina agreed, both of them were really thinking very different things.

Then Nina said, "There's something I've got to tell you. It's very important. We'll have to do something about it at once."

She found a handkerchief, blew her nose, wiped her face, and began to talk. Peter listened carefully to her somewhat incoherent story.

22

"Perhaps Mr. Thorn was wrong and it isn't in here after all," said Nina despondently after she and Peter had been searching the study for the best part of an hour.

"Well, at least it isn't in an obvious place where Dorothy can't help seeing it. I suppose that's some comfort," he replied.

"What happens when people die?" asked Nina. "I mean, what happens to things in their pockets."

"They're handed over to the next-of-kin. I don't see how you can stop Dorothy seeing it if it was in his pocket. What about somewhere else in the house?"

"It's not in the bathroom," said Nina, "and if it was in the bedroom I should think Mr. Thorn would have found it. He had plenty of time to look around. It can't be in the consulting-room because it was locked up and it can't be in the sitting-room because Mr. Thorn was there, and I was in the kitchen.

"The top floor?"

"He never goes up there. I mean, he never went up there. Gerry, I mean." Nina corrected herself, gave a great yawn, and sat down suddenly in the chair at the desk.

"I think we'd better call it a day," said Peter.

Nina did not reply. She was slumped low in the big leather-seated chair with her head drooping over the back. Her eyes were closed and she was fast asleep.

"Poor child," murmured Peter, looking down on her. It might have been Bill Thorn speaking. For a few minutes he looked around in a desultory manner at places which they had already searched and then he heard sounds of movement from the floor above. It sounded as if somebody was coming downstairs.

"I'd better go out of the back door," he said to himself, "if Dorothy doesn't want to see me now."

The thought was no less painful than it had been when it first struck him.

The following morning, which was a Saturday, Peter was staring without comprehension at a page full of diagrams and calculations, when there was a knock at the door and his heart leapt. It sounded just like Dorothy's knock when she came to call on her way home from work. When he saw Nina standing there it was all he could do to control his disappointment.

"Dorothy sends her love," said the girl as if she knew what he was feeling. "She's much better this morning but terribly busy. One of the secretaries at the hospital is coming round to write letters and make phone calls and things. There's the funeral to arrange and lots of people to tell and all sorts of other things and there's the police."

"The police," repeated Peter, feeling alarmed in spite of himself. "There'll have to be a post-mortem on Gerry, of course, but surely there's no question—"

He broke off. He saw that under Nina's determinedly bright manner the girl was very much afraid.

"They're coming to see Dorothy this morning," she said. "I suppose they'll want to see me too."

"All you do is tell them the truth. Exactly what happened," said Peter.

"I can't, I mustn't!" she cried, and yet again Peter felt that apprehensive little chill.

"Nina," he said, "has Dorothy done something that she doesn't want known? Is that why she wouldn't speak to me? Don't be afraid to tell me. I won't let her down."

Nina shook her head violently. "Not Dorothy," she said.

"Then who?"

"Mr. Thorn," she replied and burst into tears.

"I'm awfully sorry," she said after she had been revived with brandy and coffee, "you'll think I do nothing but howl on you. That's the last time, honestly. But I'll have to tell you about it now. I don't think I can tell lies to the police without someone else knowing. There's something I didn't tell you last night. He said I could tell you if I had to, but I didn't think it would be so soon. I didn't think I would be so feeble."

"You're not feeble, Nina. That's the last thing you are."

"Thanks," she said, wiping her face. "Well, here goes."

After she had finished Peter said, "I'm afraid you're going to have a tough time with the police enquiries and the inquest. But there's no need to tell any outright lie. All you have to do is not tell the full story. We'll go over it all again, with me asking questions and you answering them as you are going to do at the inquest. Ready?"

Nina was ready and performed very well.

"There you are, you see. There's nothing to it," said Peter.

But privately he was very worried, and Nina had good reason in the days to come to be grateful for his coaching.

The day after Mr, Thorn's funeral, when Dorothy and Peter and Nina were having an evening meal together at Pond Cottage, Dorothy suddenly said, in the middle of a conversation about what to do with Gerry's books, "I always used to have a good opinion of the police. But they're being so slow and stupid over Gerry's death that I'm beginning to revise it."

Peter and Nina exchanged quick glances.

"I've answered the same questions a dozen times at least," went on Dorothy. "So has Nina. And if my poor father were still alive no doubt they would be pestering him to death too. Surely they know exactly what happened by now. The autopsy was clear enough."

"I suppose they have to be very thorough," said Peter uncertainly.

"Here's your pudding," said Nina, putting a plate in front of him. "Don't wait for us. Your television programme's coming on in a few minutes."

"So it is. Thanks," said Peter.

Nina was always very anxious that he should not miss any of the relevant Open University broadcasts and that he should keep strictly to his timetable of study; but Dorothy, who had once been so helpful and encouraging, now showed only a token interest in his work. Why should she do otherwise, he said to himself; she's mourning her father; her whole life has changed completely since Gerry's death; she is coming to terms with herself. But for all his sensible arguments, it still hurt, and Nina's enthusiastic interest was comforting.

After Peter had left the room Dorothy said to Nina, "Why aren't the police satisfied? Can you think why?"

It was the question that Nina had been dreading, and she wished she had Peter's support and did not have to face it alone. She shook her head without speaking.

"It's horrible," went on Dorothy. "I feel as if Gerry is hitting back at me from beyond the grave." She looked round the kitchen as if she expected Gerry to come into the room. "He's haunting me," she went on. "I'll never be free of him."

"You'll feel better after the inquest," said Nina as soothingly as she could. "It will soon be over."

Dorothy did indeed look haunted. She went through the duties of each day in a businesslike manner, but when all demands had been met she returned to this tense and apprehensive state. It was as if she could not accustom herself to being without the menacing presence of Gerry, as if there was no way in which she could feel free.

"I feel as if he's planted a time-bomb," she said to Nina, "and that it will go off at the inquest. I can't tell you how I'm dreading it."

Nina did not know how to reply. This was so very much her own and Peter's secret dread. For Gerry's confession had never turned up, and after going into all the possibilities again and again they had come to the very unpleasant conclusion that only one thing could have happened: somehow or other Pauline Crofts had got hold of it.

"If only we knew what he'd written, or what she's told the police!" Nina cried for the twentieth time when she was alone with Peter later that evening.

"He'll have written that Dorothy was to blame for his death," said Peter.

"But they know she wasn't! Even if they don't believe me, they must believe Dr. Ferguson. She was asleep all morning. She couldn't possibly have done anything!"

"I suppose they're trying to find a loophole," said Peter wearily.

"And in any case," continued Nina, "Pauline herself saw Dorothy come out of the consulting-room half asleep. So her own evidence lets Dorothy out, doesn't it?"

"Not necessarily, I'm afraid. Dorothy could have woken earlier and come out and doped Gerry and then gone back to sleep."

"But I told them—"

"You were in the garden for quite a long time. You told them that. And Mr. Thorn is dead. There was nobody else in the house."

"But the consulting-room door was locked and I had the key!"

"Perhaps there was another key. Perhaps Mr. Thorn let her out. Or even Gerry himself."

"Peter!" Nina was indignant now. "You can't possibly suspect that Dorothy—"

"Of course I don't. I'm only pointing out how people's minds might work if they didn't know as you and I do that she is completely innocent."

"I could murder Pauline," said Nina, grinding her teeth.

"So could I. But it would be too late. The damage is done."

The inquest on the death of Gerard Laver attracted a considerable amount of attention and received wide coverage in the press. Not only did it make good human interest reading, but it was medically noteworthy too. Mr. Laver had swallowed five of his tablets when the normal dose was two at the most, but death was not due to the drug. It had been caused by hypernatraemia, haemorrhaging resulting from too much salt in the bloodstream. It could have been avoided if the dead man's father-in-law, who administered the remedy, had been aware of its dangers. And it could have been avoided if the dead man's wife, who had been suffering from nervous exhaustion, had been called earlier to her husband's aid.

For Dr. Dorothy Laver was fully aware of the dangers of this treatment for poisoning. The coroner was very interested indeed in her evidence, not because of any reflection on herself but because of its general implications. Dr. Laver explained that she had come across a similar case in the course of her work, and that on a previous occasion when her husband had taken an overdose she had been very careful about using salt water as a remedy. There had been a certain amount written on the subject, she said, but she agreed that the risks were not widely known. Dr. Ferguson, who had been called in but arrived too late, said that he himself was unaware of the danger. The coroner hoped that this case would alert people to the risks of this widely used household remedy.

When the question arose of whether any suicide note had

been found, Peter and Nina held hands tightly and held their breath. No such note had come to light, replied the police sergeant. Nina and Peter looked across to where Pauline was sitting. She was staring straight ahead of her, very red in the face.

"What can have happened?" whispered Nina to Peter when it was all over and a verdict of death by midadventure had been recorded, with a rider to the effect that the dangers of administering salt water should be widely publicized. "D'you think she never had the confession? Or didn't she tell the police about it after all?"

"Ssh," he replied. "Later."

Dorothy had joined them. She looked tired but relieved. "Well, that's that," she said. "Poor Nina. They did put you through it, didn't they? I'm beginning to think it was you whom they suspected of killing Gerry, and not me at all!"

She said this lightly but with an undertone of seriousness. It seemed a good thought to encourage, and Peter and Nina did so.

"You know, Nina, I've suspected all along that you've been hiding something," said Dorothy a little later when they were all three lingering in the garden at Pond Cottage, talking in the desultory manner of people who have gone through a dreaded ordeal and cannot quite make the transition back to their normal course of life.

"I haven't been hiding anything," said Nina in so convincingly innocent a manner that Peter's admiration for her stirred afresh. "I'd never dare to. I'm much too scared of the police. I'm a teenage delinquent, aren't I? Or I was until you rescued me."

Dorothy smiled faintly. It was hardly a happy smile, but it held a promise that the sparkle might return to her one day. "Dear Nina," she said affectionately. "We'll have to think about what you are going to do with yourself soon. Damn. There's the phone again."

"I'll go," said Nina.

But Dorothy was already running across the lawn. It was

not the first time that she had so obviously avoided being alone with Peter. She needn't have bothered, he thought rather bitterly; I'll never say anything to embarrass her.

Nina, who noticed everything, had noticed this too, and as they walked slowly after Dorothy into the house, she tried to console him.

"I don't believe she'll ever marry again," she said. "I know I wouldn't—not after being married to Gerry. It'd put anyone off for life."

"Thanks, Nina," said Peter, accepting this speech in the spirit in which it was offered.

That's another of them, thought Nina. They all thank me. It would be nice if one of them would really love me too. Although I think perhaps the old man really did love me. Her eyes stung. She could not think of Mr. Thorn without a gaping sense of loss.

"That was Pauline," said Dorothy, putting down the telephone in a rather puzzled manner. "She wants to come and see me. She says she meant to speak to me at the inquest but didn't get a chance. I suppose she wants to apologize for that ghastly business on the day Gerry died, and I must say it's about time too."

Peter and Nina silently signalled their alarm to each other.

"When is she coming?" asked Nina.

"Now." Dorothy looked at her watch. "Better make her some coffee. I'm sick to death of chatting to people and offering them cups of coffee," she added in a sudden spurt of irritation. "I'd like to get right away from it all. All the social trivia. I'd like to do something tough and unsociable and mindless. I wonder if they'd take me on an Antarctic excursion or something like that if I brushed up my general medicine a bit."

"But, Dorothy," protested Nina, "you'd never want to leave this house."

"Yes, I would. I'm sick of this house. What's a house anyway? Something to fuss over. I'd rather be in an igloo in a blizzard and fighting with something worthwhile. Or I could get in touch with the World Health people and get them to send me to somewhere really tough. There's Pauline, damn her. I'll let her in.''

In the kitchen Nina said to Peter, ''We couldn't have stopped them meeting, could we?''

''No way,'' he answered. ''But I'm beginning to wonder whether it matters that much after all. I wonder whether we haven't been underestimating Dorothy, thinking she needs our protection. The way she was talking just now, I reckon she can cope with anything.''

''I suppose,'' said Nina slowly, ''she was never really herself while Gerry was alive. I suppose she's only just beginning to turn into her real self now.''

''I wonder whether she really will go and work in a disaster area,'' said Peter. ''I should have thought Dorothy liked her comforts too much. Not that there's anything wrong with that,'' he added hurriedly. ''I like them myself.''

''People change,'' said Nina sadly.

Peter put a hand over hers. ''You're not to worry, Nina. Even if Dorothy does go off into the wilds you've still got me, for what that's worth. I won't desert you, Nina.''

''Never?''

''Never.''

''Thank you,'' said Nina.

Some time later they heard the click of the front door. ''Now for it,'' said Peter.

Dorothy came into the kitchen looking quite calm but still rather puzzled. She was holding in her hand a sheet of paper with handwriting on it.

''It's the most extraordinary thing,'' she said. ''Peter— Nina—had either of you any idea of what my father was up to?''

They both shook their heads.

''Apparently he got Gerry to sign a confession saying that it was he who gave the overdose to Irene. I can't quite see how Gerry was persuaded to, except that Dad was awfully good at getting people to do what he wanted. Anyway, Pauline found it in the study and went off with it. She's got some story about Gerry telling her there was a document he wanted her to have in the event of his death. One of his idiocies, I suppose. Anyway, she says she hadn't realized quite how mad he was until she'd taken this home and had time to digest it properly, and then she was so shocked that she couldn't make up her mind what to do—whether to tell me or whether to tell the police or what. She says that in the end she did nothing, but decided during the inquest that I ought to have this. I'm really quite glad to know. I suppose it was after he signed this that Gerry went over the edge for the last time. Well, I'm off back to work now. Thank you, both of you. For everything."

And she kissed first Nina and then Peter before she hurried away.

"Quite glad to know!" they exclaimed aloud almost in unison.

"What have we been worrying ourselves to death about?" said Peter.

"I don't trust that Pauline," said Nina. "I'm sure she said something to the police and only decided at the very last minute not to make trouble for Dorothy."

"You're probably right, but at least her better feelings came out on top in the end and she suppressed anything really harmful. Look." He held out the sheet of paper for Nina to inspect. "The bottom edge is uneven. Something's been cut off."

"Mr. Thorn was right, then," said Nina slowly. "Gerry did write something. I wonder what it was."

"I don't suppose anybody but Pauline will ever know," said Peter.